GOING DOWN MAINE

GOING DOWN MAINE

A Novel

Mark Slade

A Fortiori Enterprises

A Fortiori Enterprises
P.O. Box 2408
San Jose, CA 95109-2408

Visit our website: www.goingdownmaine.com

First U.S. Print Edition: December 2012

ISBN-13: 978-0-9885885-0-9
ISBN-10: 0988588501

Printed in the United States of America

Cover Art, Photography & Design
Morgan Riccilli Slade
www.morganskadestudio.com

There are very few with whom one holds dear... This book is wholeheartedly dedicated to...

Melinda, Morgan, Mitchel & Mikaela

The sum of behaviour is to retain a man's own dignity, without intruding upon the liberty of others...
If a man will begin with certainties, he shall end in doubts, but if he will be content to begin with doubts, he shall end in certainties.

Sir Francis Bacon

GOING
DOWN
MAINE

ONE

AT THE BEACH

David and I had something very special between us. At least, I thought so back then, when I was just Billy and not William or Bill as I am now. Hell, me an' David were going to take the world by storm! His way, of course. It was always his way. I never really minded or gave it much thought though. That is, until all of it happened and everything changed. I'm still amazed that he had such a strong hold over me and that I never saw it coming until it was too late. Maybe, it's just easier to lapse into denial. Maybe, that's why I allowed it to happen in the first place.

Another thing I wonder about - more than I should - is how tricky the human mind can be. We have this incredible capacity to block out certain events in our lives and never give them a thought for years. Then, like magic, they just pop into our heads in a flash. We can remember it all, every single instance from beginning to end. Every picture crystal clear as if we were right there experiencing it all over again. Whether we want to or not.

At certain times, I can still sense the very special smell of damp briny salt air, as it wafts up from the cream colored beach that runs along that particular New England coastline. I was always rather intrigued by the tiny wisps of summer windblown sand, as they twirled and danced over the long lazy, bleached out dunes that roll down toward the seemingly always chilly Atlantic Ocean of the upper region of Massachusetts - known to the Boston Blue Bloods as the North Shore.

As I recall, I must have been close to three and David around four or so. The Ipswich beach our parents frequented was a private stretch of sand that was off-limits to the great unwashed and only used by the local gentry, of which we were not. However, David's father's heating oil and coal trucks delivered all of the warmth during the frigid winters. And, both my father and his were members of one of the local fraternal orders of something, as their fathers had been. And, both of our mothers' maiden names were assigned to a local street and a lane - somewhere back on their family trees. Therefore, it was understood that our families were entitled to certain old money privileges. Not the least of which was the use of a private beach opposite Plum Island, which stood silent sentry beyond the surf line. Where, even at low tide, David and I were not yet old enough to battle the currents of the estuary to explore the island. So, we contented ourselves with just digging a hole in the wet sand. Not just any hole, however, since David's avid imagination was already quite active. We were digging a hole directly through the earth to China, he had exclaimed with a strong sense of unabated delight and abandon. I can still feel the nervousness in the pit of my stomach when David warned me that, if we weren't careful, we could fall all the way to China and be eaten alive by evil Chinamen!

Up on a dune just above us, the little red Irish setter pup that was David's but was understood to be mine as well - since we were best friends, jumped up through the stiff sea grass that spiked out of the sand. He tried mightily to scramble to the top of the mound. But, the soft slipping granules were more than a match for the young purebred as he tumbled down head over tail, landing flat on his soft belly at the bottom.

As the ever-searching gulls squawked above us, I watched David rapidly scoop hands full of soupy sand out of the widening hole. I scooted back from the edge, not wanting to meet an evil Chinaman, as the seawater quickly eroded the sides making the hole wider instead of deeper. I reached for my new yellow sand pail to help bail out the infiltrating water. David suddenly ripped the pail away from me and ran off into the water with the prize. I remember just sitting there for a moment. I heaved an involuntary sigh and let the large alligator tears quietly roll down my pink cheeks as David laughed, giggled, and waved my new pail at me from the surf.

Digging a hole to China or selling lemonade or playing war with my prized collection of war toys always had its price when David was involved. And, he was always involved. Our mothers, friends since birth, saw to that. Anyway, I found it easier to just let the tears roll down my cheeks. I guess my own early sense of self-preservation was still developing.

Sensing my unhappiness, the little red puppy righted himself, scampered over to me, and quickly started licking away my salty tears - trying to make it better. It worked. I reached out and hugged the soft little bundle of wiggling red fur and it was comforting.

TWO

ANCIENT STONE WALLS

It's hard for youngsters of seven and eight to envision who actually gathered and set in place the heavy glacier rocks that mark off the early farmlands of New England. David used to say that he was a distant cousin of Paul Revere, and that Paul and his friends built all the rugged stone walls around where we lived. I didn't believe him, but sometimes my friend David could be very convincing. All I do know is that we loved to race through the yellow wildflower fields, which sprang to life during our summer vacations, and jump the walls. David imagined we were riding sleek hunting horses charging across the countryside after a frightened fox, as we blew our imaginary bugles through our fists. I delighted in this game because we never caught or had to kill the fox. In fact, we never really chased a real fox ...Only Big Red.

Big Red, David's and my Irish setter, had grown up with us and could point a pheasant like an expert bird dog. Strong and steady. He could also point a gigantic butterfly, as he was doing in the middle of a flower-filled field; when his keen ears perked at the sound of our jingling bicycle bells in the distance. I saw the butterfly spiral away at his sudden movement. Big Red snapped, missed, and gave up. He whirled around and charged through the huge carpet of wildflowers toward the backcountry road that ran along the ancient stone wall bordering the field, closing fast on our approaching bikes.

In one leap, Big Red cleared the wall and fell in nose to wheel as we raced down the road. His tongue lolled out of the side of his mouth as he sprinted within inches of my spinning spokes. "Hey, Big Red! Come on! Come on, boy," we shouted together. Then, with our bathing suits and towels tied to our handlebars and snapping in the wind, David suddenly gunned his bike ahead of mine and shouted his challenge, "Last one to the bridge is a rotten egg."

I raced down the winding, tree-lined road after him. Knowing he already had too much of a head start. David was always doing this kind of contest stuff and he usually beat me because I never seemed to anticipate what he would come up with next. I guess that's what made him so much fun to be around. He always had a game going.

At the narrow country bridge, that David told me Paul Revere rode over to alert everyone that the British were coming, we jammed our bikes to a sliding stop on the dirt shoulder. Big Red leaped the guardrail and landed in the lazy river seven or eight feet below with a splash. This was a summer ritual we'd repeated time after time. Only, this particular day would be... different...

Big Red dragged himself up onto the tree shrouded riverbank and shook himself in front of the large bush where David and I were hurriedly stripping off our clothes.

David suddenly looked at me aghast. "Hey, Billy, look!" he said wide-eyed in his high-pitched voice.

"What's the matter?" I answered. Then, I noticed he was staring at my crotch. I looked down between my legs and saw nothing unusual. I looked back up at David.

"What?" I asked quizzically.

"You got one!" David announced excitedly as he pointed and stepped closer to get a better look.

"What?" I asked again and bent over myself to look at the area of my lower extremities David was indicating.

"A hair. Look. Right there," he shouted with a mixture of frustration and awe as he pressed his finger into my groin. I instinctively stepped back at his touch.

"You got a hair growing," David stated emphatically.

I looked again. "Where?" I asked.

"Right there," David answered as he hunched down to examine the area again; this time without touching me. "It's almost black, too," he mused. Then, he stood up and I realized that we were both stark naked; although, it had never occurred to me before, since we always swam naked at the river when no one else was around.

"How old are you now?" David asked me in a rather curious tone that I'd never heard before.

"You already know I'm ten. Why?" I answered and realized at the same time that my hands were cupped tightly over my genitals. Something I'd never done except when my mother came into the bathroom when I was in the tub.

"God!" David gushed.

"What's wrong?" I uttered with some alarm, gripping myself even tighter.

He stepped back. His eyes clouded, as they always did when he went into what we would later define as his 'high charge.'

"Nothing," he huffed with enough assurance that I

began to relax my painful grip and let the blood flow back. "You just started early, that's all. I hardly have any hairs at all and I'm almost eleven-and-a-half."

I quickly glanced at the bald area above David's groin and didn't see any hairs there. "Is that bad?" I asked him, not covering my apprehension very well.

"God, no! It just means you gotta learn how to use it sooner, that's all."

I tightened my grip again. "How do you know?" I asked, as a dry lump formed in my throat.

David's eyes narrowed. “My sister told me all about it," he said. Then, he sighed the way adults do when they have to begin instructing a child. “Geez, Billy, you don’t know anything do you. I'll just have to show you what to do with it, that's all."

The pain in my crotch was now excruciating. I thought I was going to pass out. "Why?" I managed to ask in a hissing rasp.

David cocked his head. "Because, my sister said when you start getting hairs that's the time to start."

My head was swimming.

"Well, do you wanna learn or not?"

I think I reluctantly nodded my head yes.

"Good. I'll go first so you can see how it works."

Over on the other side of the bush, Big Red turned in several tight circles and flopped down for a nap.

THREE

THE BOND

Big Red loped along the deserted woods-lined farm road, tongue lolling out. Knowing exactly where he was headed, he plowed right through the windswept multi-colored mounds of maple leaves that had turned and fallen - as they had every autumn since Paul Revere and his friends first cut the road through this particular forest. Then, Big Red veered off the road into the woods, picking up speed as he neared his destination.

The ramshackle chicken coop was definitely not built by Paul Revere, but was old enough to have been abandoned by several previous owners and was just perfect for David's and my secret sanctuary. "PRIVATE CLUB!" "KEEP OUT!" "NO GIRLS ALLOWED!" our hand painted, nailed up signs warned. Even though, no girls were at all interested in visiting our forgotten fortress. I mentioned once that we might change the rules to admit girls. After all, I now had two full years of experience under my belt, since my first lesson, and was definitely feeling the urge to see what else worked. David damn near nailed me to a cross over that one.

Big Red sniffed at the closed door to the club. Circled. Flopped down next to our bikes, satisfied we were inside and that all was well.

"Hold still," David demanded from inside. Big Red's ears perked as he listened.

"It's gonna hurt!" I protested with a trace of real fear in my voice.

We were seated on two old nail kegs, as a lit candle stub flickered in the center of the old wooden table in the middle of the dark chicken coop clubhouse. David was wiry and taller than most of the thirteen-year-olds around. I knew for sure, I'd never be tall, no matter how long I lived. In fact I was, most certainly, contemplating the length of my life right at that very moment, as David ran the sharp blade of his scout knife through the candle flame to sterilize it.

"It's supposed to hurt," he said with some sort of inner knowledge that I completely missed.

"What if I get blood poisoning?"

David went into his adult instructional mode. "Look," he said, "you saw me burn the blade in the candle. Here, I'll do it again, if it'll make you feel better." He did and - it didn't.

David suddenly grabbed my thumb and stabbed it before I knew what happened.

"Oh, God!" I exclaimed. Blood dripped from the tiny skin wound. "Geez, you got the bone!" I gasped in disbelief and quickly stuck the wounded thumb in my mouth to suck out the germs before gangrene set in.

David grabbed my hand and jerked my thumb out of my mouth. "Don't suck the blood, we need it. Now, shut up," he ordered. I did. I didn't know what else to do, since my heart was going to pound right through my chest - which was scaring the hell out of me.

"Okay, now I'm gonna do it to me."

David turned the knife blade in the flame. A look of fascination came over him as he gazed at the heating blade. As he withdrew it, I almost looked away, but didn't. Very slowly and deliberately, David made a small incision in his thumb. He didn't wince or show any sign of pain. He just uttered, "There," as a trickle of blood appeared and ran down his thumb.

"Oh, Jesus," I blanched.

"Gimme your thumb," David commanded.

"No!" I shot back. But, before I could retreat, David grabbed my hand and pressed the two bleeding thumbs together. He looked at me. His eyes sparkled. "There," he announced triumphantly. "Blood brothers!"

"I'm gonna be sick," I uttered weakly, knowing that it was too late to stop the blue veins from shooting up my arm full of blood poisoning.

"Come on, Billy, this is very serious," David reprimanded. Then, he leaned forward, still squeezing our thumbs together, and stared into my eyes. The candlelight flickered up onto his face. He spoke slowly in a hushed tone, as if no one in the whole world had ever heard these words before. "A bond is about to pass between us," he uttered, "a bond that no one will ever be able to take away from us." He leaned even closer. The flame danced in his eyes. "Blood brothers," he said in a hoarse whisper. I hesitated. My thumb throbbed. I could hear my heart pounding. "Say it. Blood brothers!"

"Blood brothers," I barely repeated.

"Forever!" he demanded.

I gave up. "Forever," I said. I wished I were home. But, at the same time, a certain excitement flitted through me that I'd never felt before. David's eyes sparkled again.

"Okay, now, we gotta make a wish."

"What for?" I asked, thinking the ritual was over -

thinking wrong.

"Because that's what you do when you become a blood brother."

David had this uncanny way of automatically switching out of his fantasy mode and into his instructor persona without missing a beat. "You gotta wish that the bond will never be broken and that we'll always tell each other the truth," he said. "No matter what!" he underscored. Then, switching back, "That's what blood brothers are for."

"Oh, geez," was all I could say.

"Wish," he commanded. "Wish with me, Billy. Close your eyes and wish," he intoned and closed his eyes tightly.

I looked at him with his eyes closed and the knits of extreme concentration in his forehead. My thumb was about ready to fall off. I sighed and closed my eyes just to get it over with. Besides, I'm sure David peeked at me to see if I was cooperating.

"Wish...wish hard," David said in his hushed voice, then let a long, silent moment pass before he suddenly ordered gleefully, "Okay, open."

My eyes were already open. I was never one to keep my eyes closed for long; especially when my thumb was mixing my blood with someone else's.

"Well?" David asked with heightened anticipation.

"Well, what?" I replied, not knowing what I was expected to say.

"Did you feel it?" he asked, having switched back into his fantasy mode. "Did you feel the bond pass between us?"

I knew I had to come up with some sort of reply or

the game would have gone on forever. "Yeah, I guess," I answered halfheartedly, hoping the game was over and I could take my throbbing thumb home before it fell off. I was wrong.

"Now, we gotta seal the bond with a sacrifice," David announced in the enticing tone of a mystic.

"A what?" I asked, already dreading David's answer. David leaned over the table. His eyes danced in the candlelight. "A sacrifice," he said dramatically. My heart skipped, as if I knew what was coming. "We gotta kill something," he said in a slow, measured tone. I was right.

"David..." I managed to utter in disbelief.

"No, we have to. Then the bond will really and truly be sealed." David stood up and turned to leave. "Come on, let's go," he commanded and threw open the chicken coop door.

The bright sunlight made my eyes smart as I watched David's silhouette march outside. Big Red trotted in and sniffed around. "Come on, Billy," David shouted, "hurry up!"

I sat for a moment, hoping for one last reprieve. Big Red put his paws up on my knees and licked my face. I slung my arm around his neck and listened as David tromped off into the woods. Then I blew the candle out and hurried outside with Big Red right on my heels.

The brook that ran through the woods was one of our favorite secret places. In the winter, we would spend hours after school building extensive snow villages on the ice, complete with plastic figure people and matchbox cars. David would devise an elaborate attack plan and we'd bomb the hell out of them with large rocks that would smash the snow town in a crescendo of erupting gushers of ice and water, appropriately accompanied by our exploding bomb sounds.

Summers at the secret brook offered up even better fantasies for David's special mind. Water bugs became enemies from outer space and moving targets for our laser blasters; actually, Red Rider BB guns with David's imaginative twist. Small brook trout were Russian subs. Targets for the cherry bombs we bought from some older kids and hid from our parents. Somehow, the Russian sub-trout always eluded our depth charges. Better sonar, I guess.

When Big Red and I arrived at the brook, it was almost dusk. David was hunched down on the other side of the narrow stream with his shoes off. Big Red liked the brook and sniffed everywhere. I hunkered down too, and watched David. He wasn't moving. An unsuspecting frog was sunning itself on a rock protruding out of the running water just in front of him. I watched intently. The frog jumped. David lunged and grabbed the frog in mid-flight. He rushed through the water over to me. "Gimme the string-ball, quick!" he shouted excitedly. I was the official keeper of the ball of string we always kept with us for emergencies. I quickly took it out of my pocket.

"What're you gonna do?" I asked nervously.

"You'll see," he said, holding the terrified frog tightly in his fist. "Tie the string around its legs," he ordered. I backed away. "Come on, Billy, it's important. Do it. Hurry up!"

"I...I don't want to," I said, hesitantly.

Annoyed with my anxiety, David shoved the frog at

me. "Here, you hold'im. I'll do it."

I wanted to just let the squirming frog go and forget about the whole thing; but, somehow I couldn't. David hurriedly tied the frog's legs together with the string-ball, just above its flippers. "Hold'im down on the ground," he commanded and started backing away, letting out the string from the string-ball as he went.

As I held the frog down on the damp ground, I could feel its heart pounding with fear. Just like mine did, whenever I had a bad dream that woke me up in the dark and I'd feel my pulse to see if I was still alive.

David stopped several yards away and pulled the string taut. "Okay, we're ready," he announced.

"What're you gonna do?" I asked David, as a feeling of impending doom enveloped me.

"When I give the signal, let it go."

"I don't like this, David," I protested.

"Quiet!" David ordered. "I gotta do the sacrificial prayer."

I watched silently as David looked dramatically up toward the heavens. Then, he started a chant-like prayer that I knew he was making up as he went along, but was, nonetheless, effective as hell.

"Oh, god of everlasting friendship," he began, "we offer up this living sacrifice so that the bond of blood brothers, David and Billy, will last forever!"

He stopped. His eyes rolled up into his head. David was always doing that. Just letting the whites show. He continued, letting his voice quiver, "Nothing will ever break - the bond!"

David's eyes slowly came down out of his skull and focused on the helpless frog that I had pinned to the ground. "Let it go," he ordered.

I realized what he was going to do and froze.

"Billy!" he demanded.

"No," I shot back. "Don't do it!" I could feel the petrified frog trying to free itself from my grip. I hesitated too long. David jerked the string hard. I made a grab for the frog and landed on my stomach. I lay there watching - not believing what I was seeing. David began swinging the frog around him in a long looping circle. Big Red barked excitedly from across the brook.

Again and again, David looped the frog around and around. Faster and faster. I hunched up and clutched myself tightly around my knees. I could hardly breathe as I watched the spectacle in utter amazement. Everything seemed to take on a kind of surreal feeling. Almost as if I was watching everything in slow motion without any sound, except for my own blood pounding in my ears. I was mesmerized. David's eyes shined, as he continued to whirl the frog around and around.

Then, with each loop of the string, David began to lower it. Down... down... down toward a large, flat rock just at the edge of the flowing brook. Sensing something strange, Big Red barked louder. The frog skimmed the rock and looped around again. The first sharp slap of the frog against the rock startled me. Big Red stopped barking. The succeeding slapping of the frog against the rock sickened me. I looked away, but the sickening slaps continued. I looked back at David. His adrenaline had peaked at a level that only much later would I relate to someone having a climax. Then, he stopped. Exhausted. His face glistened with perspiration and his eyes sparkled with excitement. I couldn't speak. I couldn't move. Big

Red ran over to the bloody dirt ball and anxiously sniffed all around it.

David's face was flushed almost pure white with exhilaration. He hurried over to me. I slowly stood up. David grabbed me by the shoulders. "Did you feel that?"

I felt weak. I wanted to throw up. David shook my shoulders. "Did you?" he demanded.

"Feel what?" I asked.

David looked directly into my eyes. "The sacrifice. Did you feel the sacrifice?"

All I could manage was a slight shrug. David spun away like some sort of white-faced ballet dancer and exalted dramatically to the heavens, "Now, it's done. Now the bond can never be broken. Never!"

He spun back to me. "Isn't it great," he said. "God, I've never felt anything like that in my life!"

David grabbed me by my shoulders again, harder this time. I winced as his grip squeezed into my skin. "Billy," he exclaimed, "you gotta do it too!"

I looked at him in disbelief. I felt numb all over. He loosened his grip on me and lowered his voice, "Billy, it'll make our blood bond even stronger." Then, as if to somehow reassure me - although, at that point, I don't know how that could have been possible - he spoke in a hushed, convincing tone, "It'll make it last forever."

David looked into my eyes, waiting for my reaction. Finally, I stammered, "I...it's...I gotta go home... It's getting late."

David switched to his reassuring mode again. "Okay, tomorrow," he said, then hit me with, "maybe, you could sacrifice a bird."

I stood there totally confused. My mind was

spinning like the Tilt-A-Whirl ride at the county fair. David abruptly turned away, picked up his sneakers and started back into the woods. "Come on, let's go," he called out, as if nothing had happened.

"Shouldn't we bury it?" I managed to utter.

"Why? It's only a frog. Let's go. Anyway, no one ever buries a sacrifice. They always leave it out for the gods."

He kept going. Big Red came up and rubbed against my leg, as I looked over at the dead frog lying motionless next to the flat rock.

"Are you comin' or not?" David shouted from the edge of the woods. His face still didn't have any color in it.

"In a minute," I answered.

"Last one back's'a rotten egg."

David disappeared among the birch trees. I walked over to the dead frog and hunched down over the bloody lump with its legs still tied together. Big Red gave it a quick nervous sniff and backed off, as I slowly untied the string and dug a small hole in the wet dirt next to the brook. I placed the dead frog in its little grave and covered it over.

I must have been standing there for several moments before I realized that it was getting dark. I turned away and walked into the woods with Big Red bounding on ahead.

I don't remember ever going back to the brook again after that.

FOUR

GOING DOWN MAINE

His inner-clock told Big Red that we would be at David's father's home fuel oil delivery yard, as he strode along the pristine, tree-lined street with its quaint New England houses set side by side. Some of them dated back to the 1600's, as they were so inscribed by the local historical society. We spent a lot of our summer days out on the small company yard in front of the sagging oil splattered delivery truck barns, listening to David's portable radio, while we kept his used Ford station wagon tuned up.

"She's got the biggest jugs I've ever felt!" David announced from over the car motor we were working on.

I looked up from where I was lying under the oil pan, holding a loose bracket in place. Through the tangle of distributor wires, I could just glimpse David's grease covered face and his shit-eating grin. "You didn't feel'em," I said.

"The hell I didn't," he retorted with a challenging laugh.

Sometime during the last three years, David had changed his mind about the opposite sex and now was completely obsessed with girls and their attraction to him. He dressed with them in mind and even developed a swagger of sorts. He loved being the center of their attention and never missed an opportunity to lord it over me. I guess it was a step forward from the stash of those semi-obscene big bust magazines hidden away in his attic, out of sight of his mother who was a member of the local Congregational Church choir, as was mine.

I heard Big Red leap up into the back of the station wagon where he usually took his afternoon nap if we were there. "And, I suppose you're gonna tell me you touched her snatch, too?" I teased knowing that, so far, the closest David had ever gotten to actually seeing a girl naked was by peeking under the bathroom door at his older sister taking a bath.

David stuck his greasy middle finger down through the distributor wires and wiggled it in my face. "Wanna smell?" he joked.

I couldn't help laughing and shoved his hand away. Even though we had both matured, David still had that glint of mischievous danger in his eyes that was his disarming and charismatic charm. I, on the other hand - although I wasn't aware of it at the time - seemed to attract the glances of the local girls; but, at fifteen, didn't realize what I had going for me and was content to let David front for us.

"I was looking in the rearview mirror the whole time and all I saw was a bunch of French kissing and her pushing your hand away."

"God, no wonder you never get any. You're always lookin' at what I'm doin'," David said.

"Just keeping the record straight," I replied.

David went into his evil-eyed-monster act. "Anyway, de-hand-ees-queeker-zan-zee-eye," he seethed, rolling his tongue lasciviously over the words. "De poor thing had no control over zee lightening fast magic finger of DAH-veed zee magnificent!"

"You're crazy," I laughed.

He opened his eyes extra wide and lisped fiendishly, "Yeth, I know."

We finished our work and quickly went about putting the tools away. David was a couple of inches taller and much thinner; and, even though I was a year and a half younger, I already had more muscular definition than David and was being scouted by the varsity football coach for the coming season. This situation was a source of silent irritation with David who had bragged to anyone who'd listen that he was going to be the first string quarterback and I would be his end. So far, the varsity coach had only seen some muscular potential in me and nothing more. Therefore, I just didn't deal with it. It was still summer, and hell, David and I were going down Maine.

"Let's get cleaned up and hit the road before dark," David said, as we walked out of the yard.

David's house was right across the street from the family business. I lived around the corner. "I'll pick you up in half an hour," he said and let out a sharp whistle. Big Red leaped from the back of the station wagon and beat David to the front of his house where he whined excitedly to be let in.

"I gotta make sure Big Red's inside so he won't follow us," David said.

"Why can't he come with us?"

"He'll just get in the way," David answered and headed up the walkway to the white clapboard house that had been in his family for three generations. In fact, the old chain link swing that was his father's as a child still hung from a limb of the giant chestnut tree that David's great grandfather planted next to the house. Just goes to show how people around these parts desperately hang onto traditions large and small.

My own family was very much steeped in the traditional New England ways of life. Carved pumpkins exactly seven days before Halloween. Giblet gravy and hard sauce at Thanksgiving. A locally harvested blue spruce tree at Christmas. And, yellow crocuses every spring. My father took over my grandfather's downtown insurance business, which made everyone feel very comfortable, knowing that particular tradition would be carried on without a hitch - along with the annual Premium increases.

Dad was a rather quiet man and conscientious way beyond the call of duty, which meant that he missed most of my Little League games and father-son fishing trips were few and far between. But, everyone in town liked Dad and so did I.

Mom, on the other hand, was something to behold. A tiny bundle of pure energy who, having been born a fifth cousin to a founding family name that had long ago been allocated to a local street sign, felt it her inherent duty, obligation, and mission in life to be at the beck and call of every charity and volunteer group that our small town could produce. Being taken advantage of was more like it. But, the load of work she took on only made her strive for more, a fault which not even I could argue with. However, being the only child of parents who believed in doing unto others and living by the Golden Rule did have its drawbacks. They insisted that being fifteen meant I couldn't drive a car because I wasn't old enough to have a driver's license. My not being sixteen meant that David did most of the driving in his used station wagon; although, I sometimes drove to the drive-in movie when David wanted to use the back seat as his personal passion pit.

Driving with David at the wheel was an experience unto itself. Wherever we drove, David would chatter endlessly about anything that came into his labyrinthine mind, sometimes ignoring the road altogether when he was making one of his all-important points. This would be our first trip together without our parents, neither his nor mine. And, getting to this point of actually hitting the road had taken six months of intense lobbying on both our parts. I guess it's all a matter of trust with parents and their children, with the children not trusting in the seemingly indelible parental scriptures and parents just not trusting their kids at all - with good reason. Although, my folks weren't all that hard to convince; it was David's parents who were the most difficult to crack.

His father was always an enigma to me. The only person I've ever met who seemed to have no personality whatsoever. I never saw him laugh or tell a joke or even get mad at David. He hardly ever spoke to David's mother when I was around. As a matter of fact, he hardly ever spoke to me. He'd just walk across the street every morning at seven o'clock and go into his little office at the fuel oil company and close the door. We wouldn't see him again until five, when he'd leave the office and walk, a little unsteady, back across the street to his house.

When David asked him if we could drive to Maine by ourselves, he just referred the decision to David's mother. So, it was left up to David's continuous banging on his mother's psyche that finally bore the fruits of victory and we were on our way down Maine with David's station wagon packed with our sleeping bags, suitcases, a cooler full of ice, and enough food to feed a small army.

As we drove along a back road, just outside of town, David was doing a rather unkind imitation of his mother, who was forever doting on her only son. "Did you remember your poison ivy pills?" he asked in his mother's very New England nasal twang. "And, your sun block?"... "Yes, Ma," he answered, switching to himself.

I had to laugh, even though he was being very cruel. I happened to like David's mother. However, I didn't have to live with her as he often pointed out to me.

"I talked with your father," David twanged on, "and he said not to forget to shut off the water in the cottage when you leave... Yes, Ma...and, don't let Billy drive that car. He doesn't have his license yet... Yes-Ma-Yes-Ma-Yes-Ma," David shouted out with a sense of real frustration mixed in with his comic routine.

"Cut it out. She's not that bad," I said through my laughter.

"God, she even tried to squeeze my zit before I could get out of there! Can you imagine that?"

I tried not to.

Suddenly, David swerved into the woods onto a rutted dirt lane that I'm sure was definitely used by Paul Revere. At least, it seemed as if no one had tried to keep it in repair since Paul made his ride. The dates on the ancient grave markers in the forgotten graveyard, where the lane led to, went back to Revere's time and before. In fact, I've been told that our family had a distant cousin buried there who was killed at Bunker Hill. I wonder what he'd think, knowing that he fought for the right for modern day teenagers to make love on top of his grave on hot summer nights.

Anyway, as David drove too fast over the ruts, I turned around and adjusted our suitcases that had shifted in the back of the wagon. We were only planning to stay at David's folk's summer cottage on the Maine coast for about a week, but had enough stuff for a month it seemed. Although David had been on quite a few trips to Maine with his parents, I had only been there one other time, about seven years before, but only remembered that it was a long trip and was somewhere south of New Brunswick and Campobello Island where the Roosevelt family used to summer. I also remember that there weren't too many people around and David and I got pretty bored after awhile. David had assured me emphatically that this time it would be different. Much different.

"Promise me you'll be careful," David twanged like his mother again. "Yes, Ma. I promise, Ma...I..."

"There's the cemetery," I said and David swerved off the lane into the overgrown graveyard with its blackened, fungus-covered markers stabbing eerily up through the high grass.

"This place gives me the creeps," I said.

David stopped the car and jumped out. "This is where my sister lost her cherry," he announced.

I got out, too. "Great," I uttered.

David ran behind a large granite gravestone that marked the last resting place of a woman who died in 1814, at the age of thirty-one. David had summarized that she was a prostitute because the inscription on the headstone read, "She fell by the wayside and the angels took her home." I didn't argue David's conclusion about the dead woman's profession. As a matter of fact, I felt rather sorry for her.

"TA-DAH!" David trumpeted as he appeared from behind the prostitute's gravestone, hefting two cases of Budweiser.

It wasn't hard for a teenager to get beer where we lived. There were plenty of older brothers hanging around with nothing better to do. And, there was the half blind old lady who ran the seedy secondhand shop in the next town. She was only too happy to sell beer to any kid who could scrape together three times the price and show her a phony I.D. It didn't seem to matter how phony either. David was just seventeen and had reddish hair. The photo on his I.D. had a guy with a black mustache about twenty years older.

"Open the tailgate," David said, as he lugged the beer toward the back of the station wagon.

As I opened the hatch, I heard a loud noise of something crashing toward us through the woods. David stopped in his tracks. "What the hell's that?"

I looked toward the sound coming from beyond the old stone wall that surrounded the graveyard. We both froze at the sight of the large red blur leaping over the wall right at us.

"Oh, shit!" David blurted out, almost dropping the two cases of beer.

Big Red nearly knocked me to the ground as he jumped through the air and landed in the back of the station wagon. He instinctively licked my face as his tail thumped excitedly against the inside window.

"Goddammit," David said, "we're gonna have to take'im back."

"No we don't."

"Are you kidding? He'll follow us all the way up there. This's the fuckin' pits."

"We'll just bring'im with us," I said, patting Big Red's head.

David shoved the cases of beer into the car. "We can't. He'll spoil everything. He'll get lost or something."

"He won't get lost," I protested, "he's a dog. We'll stop at a phone and tell your mother he's with us, that's all."

David thought for a moment. Something he didn't usually do. "Shit. Okay-okay, let's go."

Before David changed his mind, I quickly shut the back of the station wagon. As David wheeled out of the graveyard, Big Red nuzzled me from the back seat and licked my face profusely. His way of saying thanks.

Most people who travel through the upper New England states - Massachusetts, New Hampshire, Vermont, Maine - come away with eloquent surface descriptions of how quaint and picturesque the string of small Puritan towns are, and how spectacular the colors are that paint across the trees in the autumn of the year. That's what most people do. I, on the other hand, have often wondered why it is that New Hampshire license plates proclaim the quite ominous state slogan, "Live Free or Die." Or, why the long established families of Maine look at any first generation resident as an "outsider." Vermont, so I've heard, has a town full of people with genetically pointed heads; although, I don't know anyone personally who has actually visited this particular place.

However, David swore on his grandmother's grave that it's true. He told me that it had something to do with different sects leaving the original Salem settlements to escape religious persecution and then intermarrying to keep their sect pure. David had a head full of this kind of knowledge, which I never questioned that much. I just filed most of it away as fiction, until I found out if any of it was fact. Then, of course, Massachusetts used to be identified with the Kennedys - something the Chamber of Commerce promoted with a vengeance during "Camelot." Not so much, nowadays.

"Why do we say, 'going down Maine' instead of 'going up Maine'?" I mused out loud to David as we crossed over the border between New Hampshire, "The Granite State" and Maine, "The Pine Tree State." I shouldn't have asked. The history lecture that followed took almost half an hour and had something to do with the early trading ships having the wind at their backs when they sailed from Boston to Maine – when Maine was a territory before it was a state. So, they were sailing downwind, hence the term, "going down Maine." I bought the story just to get out of class.

"How'bout a couple'a beers, mate?" David asked cheerily, as we raced north over the wood shrouded highway.

I broke out of my thought-trance and reached into the back where David had stashed the beer. As I ripped open a case, Big Red raised his sleepy head, looked at me and dozed off again, content that he was along for the ride.

"Hey, watch it ass-wipe!" David shouted, as beer sprayed all over the dashboard and windshield when I opened the pop-top.

"It's warm," I snapped, wiping the dash with my baseball cap.

"No shit, Dick Tracy. Put some in the cooler."

I handed the opened beer to David and rolled down my window and popped my beer into the wind. The old New England towns, with their small white Christian churches, were left behind as the miles ticked off and I popped more cans into the wind. We were feeling great. On our own. Going down Maine. No parents! The two original members of the chicken coop club. Bonded in blood for life. Singing and shouting rock'n'roll with abandon to the blaring car radio.

It was pitch black, and a six-pack later, when our bladders hit the wall. David braked to a sliding stop on the shoulder of the deserted Maine turnpike. All three of us sprang from the car. David and I relieved ourselves with great sighs and groans, silhouetted in the bright headlights. Big Red, being much more discreet, found a bush and did what he had to do.

"Goddamned beer goes right through you," David announced, as the sounds of water spraying on dead leaves came from three different locations.

We got back into the car and drove off into the night, heading north. I fell asleep.

FIVE

WELCOME TO PEAKSPORT

...The time between dreaming and waking can be jarring as hell, sometimes. Especially, if you're caught in some gray, colorless inner void and are being chased by a throng of ghostly beings, with pointed heads, who are led by a huge frothing, black-and-white mutant. There's no feeling in your right leg. No chance whatsoever of outrunning the grisly freaks. Holy shit! Where's Paul Revere when you need him?...

Suddenly, David's voice echoed with great enthusiasm from somewhere outside the void. "This is it," he shouted.

The early morning sun blasted right through my window into my eyes. For one brief moment, I thought I was dead. Then, I wished I was. My head had a huge railroad spike hammered right through it. Beer always did that to me. Never to David, who could drink two six-packs, stay up all night, and be ready to hit the ground running at the first sign of some action. I just tried to keep up and paid the price. I squinted in the bright sun and slapped my tingling right leg, which had jammed up against the door and had fallen asleep. My mouth tasted like Big Red had pissed in it.

"Isn't it great," David said.

I squinted through my throbbing eyeballs. David had stopped on the crest of the pine-studded road that looked down onto an isolated coastal fishing village nestled along a mountain encircled cove. A dozen or so gray-weathered shingled buildings, hung with lobster buoys and drooping shrimp nets, comprised the main part of town. There were piles of wooden slotted lobster traps everywhere. I naturally assumed this was the growth industry up - I mean 'down' - here.

Several old lobster boats were tied up to the one sagging pier that jutted into the placid cove where a few shrimp trawlers were moored. A peaceful early morning mist was rapidly burning off the dark sparkling water. It looked like one of those tranquil color photographs out of National Geographic.

"That's it?" I managed to utter. It looked much smaller than I'd remembered it. But, there was no way my condition could dampen David's enthusiasm.

"Yeah, the thriving metropolis of Peaksport, Maine," he announced like some sort of official greeter. All I wanted to do was drink a gallon of ice water and go to bed.

"It looks dead," I said.

"Are you kidding? There's more pussy down there than in twenty cities!" David had this habit of associating almost everything with the female anatomy.

"Sure," I muttered. I wasn't interested in anything at the moment. My entire body hurt.

"Man, there's nothing else to do up here but fuck. And, do these hicky girls put out."

David was in heaven. I was in hell. "Where's the cabin?" I moaned.

David pointed, "Over the other end of town, back up in the woods overlooking the cove." Then, David started driving down the pothole-patched road toward the town - such as it was.

We passed an old rotting sign, WELCOME TO PEAKSPORT, MAINE, POP. 188. I wondered, within the cobwebs of my mind, what kind of fun we could possibly have in a town with one hundred and eighty-eight people.

Suddenly, Big Red started barking furiously at something outside the car. I looked around. "Holy shit!" I blurted out.

"What?" David asked, startled.

"Look at that," I answered, dismayed at the sickening sight of the bone-skinny, rabid, mottled stray dog standing by the side of the road, shivering uncontrollably, gobs of white foam dripping from its gaping mouth.

"Gross!" David exclaimed and sped away.

I looked back and saw the pathetic creature try to hobble forward. Delirious. Out of its mind. I was glad we were leaving it behind for someone else to deal with. I also hoped it wouldn't be joining up with the pointy-headed freaks in my dream.

"Watch this," David announced, as we entered the town. He turned off the ignition and coasted silently past the old wooden buildings. The place looked deserted, except for a grizzled old fisherman watching us from one of the lobster boats tied up to the sagging dock. I thought I saw him spit a big tobacco loogie into the water as we drove by.

The loud bang from the car's backfire scared the

crap out of me. I'd momentarily forgotten David's trick of turning off the ignition, letting the fumes build up in the exhaust system, and then quickly turning the car back on so the fumes would explode. It didn't do much for the muffler, but we had a lot of fun scaring girls, dogs, and old ladies back home. It was lucky David's father went to high school with our Police Chief and undercharged him for his winter heating oil. David laughed all the way through the town. I managed a chuckle, even though my head was splitting in half. Big Red just wagged his tail and panted impatiently in the back of the car. He probably couldn't wait to find a tree.

The small, neat, white clapboard cottage was just as David had described it to me and sort of how I'd remembered it. Set back in the circle of thick pines on a bluff that overlooked the cove below. As David drove - no, barreled was more like it - up the narrow dirt road toward the cottage, he began singing an old camp song at the top of his lungs. I joined in as best I could. "We're-here-because-we're-here-because-we're-here-because-we're-heeeeeere-We're-here-because-we're-here-because-we're-here!"

David jammed on the brakes, in his best action-adventure style, right in front of the cottage. He jumped from the station wagon and threw his arms into the clean, fresh Maine air. "Bring on the broads!" he shouted to the heavens. As if all three of them would come running out of the woods to kneel at his feet. I was right about Big Red. He leaped from the back of the car, over me, and hit the nearest tree with a steady yellow stream. I got out and looked around. There wasn't another house in sight. Just thick pine woods surrounding the neat little cottage.

Miraculously, my youthful immune system was kicking in and the fog was lifting in my head.

"Hey, this isn't bad," I said.

"Are you kidding? It's the one great move my father ever made - except for having me, of course."

"What do we do now?" I asked.

David looked at me as if I had two heads. "What do we do now?" he mimicked, and then went into his sarcastic instructor mode just to crank me up. "We stow the goodies, open a beer, and wait. That's what we do now."

"Wait for what?" was my natural inquiry.

David looked at me with a secretive glint in his hazel eyes. "You'll see." Then, he abruptly turned back to the station wagon. "Let's get unpacked," he commanded.

Big Red rubbed up against my leg, then started sniffing all around, leaving his mark as he cordoned off his territory.

The inside of the cottage was just as clean as the outside. David's mother had decorated the place in traditional plaids and colonial checks. There was a small stone fireplace in the tiny living room, with a supply of chopped wood and newspapers to start a fire if the evenings were nippy, and a Franklin stove in the kitchen to ward off cool mornings.

I dumped our sleeping bags, suitcases, and David's portable radio on the twin beds in one of the two bedrooms. David was already stashing the beer and food in the refrigerator. He shouted to me from the kitchen that was just off the living room. "Hey, man. Let's eat. I'm starved." That meant only one thing. I was being designated chief cook for the duration, which was okay with me. David tried his hand at cooking once and nearly burned his house down. From that time on, he was only allowed to make sandwiches with cold cuts, but even failed at that. Besides, the spike wound in my head had dramatically healed and my own stomach was growling.

"More food! More food!" David ordered through a mouthful of scrambled eggs and bacon that he slugged down with a gulp of Budweiser, instead of the orange juice I'd mixed up in one of his mother's pitchers.

"Who made you camp counselor?" I protested.

"Hey, it's what you do best. You do all the cookin' and I'll do all the screwin'," David chortled.

"Yeah-right," I retorted, as I set what was left on my plate onto the floor for Big Red, who was more than happy to lick it clean.

Then, David suddenly stood straight up from the table and issued an order like an Army drill sergeant. "If we're gonna be in shape to take on what this new world has to offer, we gotta get some Z's." He was right. All the beer and food and very little sleep had nearly exhausted all my adrenaline reserves.

We crashed onto the twin beds without unpacking and I quickly drifted off into a deep sleep – wondering what this 'new world' had to offer.

BANG!... *What-the-hell-was-that...* I sat bolt upright on the bed, just as Big Red skittered out of the room, barking his loud protective warning bark, as he had always done when he sensed immanent danger. He'd left so fast, he'd knocked my suitcase off the ladder-back chair I'd set it on. I swung my legs over the side and almost tripped on the braided rug that Big Red's sudden launch had sent rippled up next to the bed. David wasn't in the room. Big Red was barking from the living room.

"What's wrong with him?" I asked as I hurried into the kitchen where David was feeding his face again.

"Probably an animal," David answered. "Knock it off," he ordered Big Red.

Big Red responded and quieted to a low, threatening growl. I went into the living room and looked out the front window. An uncomfortable twinge hit me in the pit of my stomach. Leaning against the station wagon was a scrawny, hollow-eyed kid who had a somewhat simple look. He was dressed in shabby clothes and stared right back at me with beady little eyes that were too close together. I called back to David who was still stuffing his face in the kitchen, "Hey, there's someone out there."

"Who?" David asked through his mouthful of potato chips.

"How should I know? There's some weird lookin' kid leaning on the car."

David jumped up from the kitchen table and charged into the living room. He looked quickly out the window. "Hey, it's Petey Peak," he announced excitedly. "He's right on time."

"Who is..." I started ask, but David was already opening the front door.

"I told you all we had to do was wait," he said to me and flung the door open.

David ran out of the cottage and right up to the peculiar looking kid. "Hey, Petey," David greeted.

Big Red ran outside and skidded to a stop. He growled low at the stranger, then put his tail between his legs and slunk a safe distance away. The sallow-faced kid watched Big Red for a moment. His expression never changed and he didn't speak.

"How you been, Petey?" David prompted.

Petey just nodded and looked past David at me standing quietly in the open doorway. David followed Petey's gaze. "Oh, that's my friend, Billy," David said and introduced me. "Hey, Billy, this is Petey Peak."

"Hi," I uttered with reservation.

Petey cocked his smallish head and looked me over from top to bottom. The feeling in my stomach churned up again.

"Petey's gonna be our guide," David announced to me. "He knows everything that's goin' on around here. Right, Petey?"

Petey just nodded slowly, without taking his little raisin eyes off me. My headache was coming back.

"Hey, Petey, remember that girl with the dark hair?" David asked. "She still around?"

Petey nodded. David's eyes lit up. He walked back to me and whispered, "Man, there's a girl up here with tits as big as watermelons and I'm gonna nail'er!" He then turned back to Petey. "You wanna beer?" Petey nodded and followed David into the cottage. As he passed me, I caught a whiff of Petey Peak and almost gagged up my bacon and eggs. Big Red waited until we had all gone into the kitchen before he entered the house. He watched suspiciously from the living room.

Petey slumped into a chair at the kitchen table. I stood downwind of our local tour guide, as protection against heaving up my breakfast. David popped three beers, handed them out and sat opposite Petey. "So, what's goin' on, Petey? Anything happening? Billy's horny."

"Hey!" I protested to David. I was far from being sexually aroused.

David laughed at me then asked Petey, "Anything going on tonight?"

Petey sipped his beer and dug at something in his short, matted, dishwater blond hair. He looked at me again with his dull, haunted eyes. Then, he looked back at David and finally spoke in a flat, emotionless, nasal twang that is particular to the upper Maine backwoods region. "Nuthin' much... Jes' tha dance ov'ah ta tha bahn."

"Hey, great," David responded brightly. And to me he said, "Man, I'll show you something you've never seen before."

"What?" I inquired. I really didn't know if I wanted to see much more, because I was certain that I would now be adding Petey Peak to my dream.

"You'll see," David answered mysteriously. "It's just a little game Petey showed me last summer. Right, Petey?"

Petey found what he was digging for in his scalp and examined it. He grinned at the discovery and exposed a row of yellow rotten teeth, as he squeezed whatever it was between his skinny, dirty fingertips and flicked it away. I was positive the drooling rabid dog was his pet.

"What kind of game?" I asked David.

He snickered, "Never mind. You'll see tonight. What'll we do today, Petey?"

I persisted, "You never told me about any game."

David's eyes flashed a look I hadn't seen for several years. It disturbed me. I suddenly recalled a time at the brook. "I never told you about a lot of things," he snapped and looked directly into my eyes... *the frog!...the frog!...* Then, he quickly brightened. "Hey, let's go downtown. We need some shells for the hunt," he announced.

Before I could ask, "What hunt?" David was already beating it out the front door. Petey sat there grinning at me. His beady eyes locked on mine. I hurried after David.

As David drove away from the cottage, I rolled down my window to mix fresh air with the aroma coming from Petey - the tour guide from hell - who was sitting in the back seat of the station wagon. I could feel his little BB eyes on the back of my head. "Come on, David, what're you talkin' about? What hunt?"

David nimbly changed the subject. "Are you sure you locked Big Red in the house?"

"Yes. Come on, will you? What's going on?"

I saw David catch Petey's eye in the rearview mirror. A secretive grin crossed David's face.

"Okay. Big hairy deal," I said, "who cares anyway." I was used to this kind of wait me out stuff from David. He'd been doing it to me since we were little. The only problem was I could never wait long enough to win.

"Billy's-mad-and-I'm-glad-and-I-know-what'll-please-him," David teased.

"Blow off," I snapped and looked out the window at the passing pine trees, determined to wait David out this time.

"Okay. Don't be such a hard-ass, we're taking you on your first skunk run," David said. "I know you've never been on a skunk run before."

I couldn't believe it. David quit before I had. "What the hell's a skunk run?" I asked, feeling I'd one-upped him - I hadn't. I saw the glint come back into his eyes.

"You'll see. Right, Petey?" I looked around at Petey,

who was grinning at me with his yellow teeth.

It only took about four minutes to get into the little town, but I was already in a black mood and not ready for anymore of David's stupid mind games. I think he sensed it, because he pulled up in front of the dilapidated country store without saying another word. It was one of those shack-type places covered with rusting metal advertising signs of old products like Lifebuoy Soap and Moxie - the kind of place that would win a black and white photo contest in the old Life Magazine. The kind of place I like to avoid whenever possible.

As we piled out of the station wagon, I glanced around for the rabid dog. Fortunately, it was nowhere in sight; so I followed David and Petey up onto the creaky wooden boardwalk and into the dimly lit store. Just as advertised, it was rundown and filthy, with clutter and years of grime everywhere. The place was quiet and seemed deserted. David leaned over the wooden counter and called out toward an open door to a back room, "Anyone here?"

The spooky place was divided by two rows of unpainted shelves that held a sparse selection of canned goods and some packaged food, mixes, and flour. I was certain they were living quarters for hordes of weevils and roaches. A craggy, skinny old man shuffled out of the back room and approached the counter. His hair was short fuzz and his skin was sallow-gray. He had the same hollow look as Petey. He looked suspiciously at David and me.

"Hi," David said brightly.

The old man just nodded slightly. No expression.

"Remember me?" David asked. "I was in here last summer with my folks. We own the cottage up in the pine grove."

The old guy just nodded again. No expression. David jacked his thumb in my direction. "That's my friend Billy. We're up here for a few days."

"Hi," I said to the expressionless old man. He just looked me up and down the way Petey had done. I figured it was some sort of backwoods, subhuman ritual or something.

"Ah, I need some .22 long rifles," David said to the old man.

"How many?" the man uttered in the same low twang that Petey spoke with.

David started to answer, "Ah..."

"Skunk run?" the man interjected.

"Yeah-right," David answered with a hint of surprise in his voice.

The grizzled old man took a box of .22 long rifle bullets from the dusty shelf behind him and placed them on the counter in front of David. "Anythin' else?" he twanged.

"No, I don't think so. Yeah, some ice for our cooler," David answered.

"Dog food," I remembered.

"Right," David agreed. "I forgot. You got any dog food?" he asked the man.

The old guy pointed a bony finger toward the other end of the small store. "T'othah side a-them they-ah shelves," he said.

"I'll get it," I said quickly - wanting to get the hell out of there.

I walked to the other side of the second row of shelves and started looking for the dog food, when something caught my eye. Something was moving slightly in a darkened corner. I froze in stark terror at what I saw seated in an old overstuffed chair. My breath caught in my throat! I could only stare wide-eyed with fear at one of the most horrible sights I'd ever seen. There, almost hidden in the shadows, was something awful. Something almost not human. What must have been a young man, at one time, was a disfigured mass of ugly flesh. Almost unrecognizable as a human being. Half his face had been blown away. Lumps of pink scar tissue and splotches of dark hair covered his mottled skull. He was staring at me with his one wild eye. I heard his breath coming in low rattling gasps. Horrified beyond belief, I started backing away.

"Hey, where's the dog food? We gotta get goin'," David said to me, as I backed around the shelves and turned to him. I felt cold and weak and could hardly move.

"What's the matter with you?" David asked me. "You look like you've seen a..." Something stopped David. Someone was coming up behind me. I stood frozen in place. I heard the shuffling noise pass within inches and felt the hairs bristle on my neck. My eyes darted to the dark form of the disfigured man, as he dragged his weak legs toward the front door. He stopped for a moment, as if to look around at me. He didn't and slowly shuffled out of the store. I stared after him in shocked silence.

Suddenly, David burst out laughing. "Hey, Billy," he croaked, "haven't you ever seen a fucking zombie before?"

My whole body was trembling.

"Cut it out," I snapped.

David stopped laughing and turned back to the

counter to pay for the ammunition. "It's just Petey's cousin, Cyrus Peak, that's all."

Petey grinned wide at me and picked at his hair.

"What...what happened to him?" I managed to ask.

"He stood up on the machine gun course in Basic Training in the Army and got blasted," David explained. "He's just a vegetable now. Get the dog food, so we can get goin'."

I just stood there for a moment, knowing full well that another monstrosity would be invading my dream.

As we came out of the store, I stopped and watched the crippled Cyrus Peak hobble down the street. A scrawny dog, picking through a toppled trash can, chased after him nipping at his old black boots. The pathetic cripple didn't seem to notice.

David gunned the car engine and shouted at me, "Will you come on!"

Still watching after Cyrus, I carried the bags of dog food and ice to the station wagon and got in. David squealed a U-turn and roared back toward the cottage.

"What'd he stand up for?" I asked David as he turned off the main road.

"Because, he's a dumb shit, that's why."

I looked back to see Cyrus, but we were already speeding up the bumpy wooded road toward the cottage.

Back at the cottage, Big Red avoided Petey and found the tree he'd already marked as his outdoor rest stop. David called to Petey, as he carried two six-packs of beer from the cottage. "Open the tailgate," he ordered. Petey opened the gate and David put the beer on ice in the cooler, then called over to me where I'd found my own tree to relieve myself on. "Hey, Billy, train's leaving. Put Big Red back in the house."

Too late. Big Red, sensing he was going to be left behind again, leaped into the back of the open station wagon. I guess he'd decided that even he could stand Petey Peak's stench, if it meant he could come along. I wasn't in such a hurry as I lingered by the tree and thought about not going with them.

"God, will you get your mind off that dummy," David called to me from the car. "We came up here to have a good time. Let's go. I've got something that'll really blow your mind."

I got into the car, thinking that my mind had been blown enough for one day.

"I mean, I'm gonna show you a sight you've never seen before," David emphasized as he started the engine. "Right, Petey?" Petey nodded and grinned and shot me a look from the back seat.

David wheeled around and drove away from the cottage. "What now?" I asked.

"Prepare yourself for the most beautiful sight you've ever seen," David announced dramatically. "We're going where no man has ever tread."

"What about the shells you bought?" I asked.

"What about'em?" David answered coyly.

"What're you gonna put'em in?"

"Look under the seat."

I reached under the seat, felt something and gingerly pulled out David's .22 rifle that he was only allowed to use with his father. "Again," David commanded. I reached under the seat and touched something cold – steel – a well used .22 Colt pistol.

"Geez! Where'd you get this?"

"Over in Slumtown, two weeks ago. It only cost me fifty bucks."

I turned the blue steel pistol in my hands. "God, that's illegal. What'd your parents say?"

"Are you kiddin' me? My father would have a shit-fit-hemorrhage if he knew. I hid it in that old club house we used to have in the woods."

I continued to turn the pistol in my hands. "Geez..." I uttered.

"Which one do you wanna use?" David asked me.

"For what? What're we gonna shoot?"

David looked at me with his quirky sidelong glance. "The skunk run, mah-man, I told you."

I hesitated for a moment; then asked, "Is that where we're going now?"

"No. Not until it gets dark," David answered nonchalantly.

I hefted the pistol for a moment more; then put it and the rifle back under the seat. All this and we had only been in picturesque Peaksport, Maine for half a day.

SIX

THE VIRGIN FOREST

The back road David was taking had narrowed to almost a single lane and didn't look like it was used much. The dense forest on both sides was so thick; it felt like we were going through a tunnel. David slowed down next to one of those ancient stone walls like the ones that Paul Revere and his farmer friends built back home. Up ahead, there was a sort of broken down entrance to the forest, probably where a road used to be. David pulled up to the entrance and stopped the car. I looked out at the thick forest. It was very quiet and quite dark beyond the first few rows of pine trees. I don't know why a feeling of foreboding hit me at the time, but it did.

"Here we are," David said mysteriously, adding to my uneasiness.

We all got out of the car. Big Red certainly didn't feel anything ominous about the forest. He was thrilled at the sight of all the big trees to choose from and made the most of it.

"Well? What am I supposed to see?" I asked David. My sarcasm was intentional.

...As a point of fact, I'd picked up a rather pessimistic edge about a year before; when, for the first time, I really became attracted to one particular girl - as opposed to girls in general. Patricia was her name. She wasn't the prettiest girl in our freshman class; but there was something about her that gave me a certain feeling whenever I saw her. She wasn't new to the area. I'd just never noticed her before. Up until then, I was always too busy running around with David to notice much of anything. She sat two seats in front of me in Ancient History class. The only class I had without David.

I first noticed her arms. The only part of her I could see from my seat near the back of the room. They were lean and muscular and had a rather tawny hue, even in the middle of winter. Rather unusual for our neighborhood, whose lineage was nearly all Paul Revere, as far as I knew. I later learned that she was Italian, which made sense. She lived over near the old colonial fishing port side of town, where quite a few Italian families had settled early on. However, that had nothing to do with why I was attracted to her. It was her silence. She seemed to walk alone among the rest of us. It wasn't that she was unfriendly or anything; she just seemed to be apart somehow, even when she was in a group.

Anyway, this feeling inside me began to take hold and I finally got up enough courage to pull the oldest and dumbest trick in the book. I dropped a pencil next to her desk and caught her eye. I smiled at her. She smiled back. That did it. I had to carry my books and binder over my crotch for the rest of the day.

It took me two weeks to make any contact beyond our occasional smiles at each other and I was running out of pencils. I was working on a term paper about the significance of the Crusades and had to look up something in the school library after school. Just as I was about to open the library door, I saw her through the door window sitting alone at one of the long study tables surrounded by opened books. My heart leaped! I walked around in circles outside the door, like Big Red did before he'd lie down. Then, I finally sucked it up and went in.

Except for Patricia, the library was empty. Not a surprise, given that everyone in school was out of there like a shot at the sound of the final bell, so they could get the best seats at Vic's pepper steak shop. In fact, had it not been for my term paper, I would have been there with David watching him stud it up in front of the freshman girls.

I went right to the shelves and pretended to search for a book. I glanced over at Patricia to see if she was looking at me, but she was too engrossed in making her notes. I quickly jerked a book from a shelf - I didn't realize it was a children's abridged version of *The Adventures of Tom Sawyer* - and sat quietly opposite Patricia at the study table. She looked up and smiled. I smiled back. I was glad I was seated because I could feel the blood rushing through my body. I pretended to read the book in my hands. I looked up again. She was staring right at me. Her eyes were twinkling, almost black. Her hair was dark, with an auburn glow that seemed to radiate in the late afternoon sun that shined through the library windows. It took me a full minute to realize that there was laughter in her eyes. And, she was quietly laughing at me. She gestured to the book in my hands. Not only was I reading a children's book, I was reading it upside down!

I walked Patricia from the library to the bus stop where we waited for her cross-town bus in the winter chill of the afternoon. I did most of the talking. Not the usual boasting kind that David always did. I sort of discussed my parents. The movies I liked. Television shows. Big Red. Things like that. I told her I might be going out for varsity football, but hadn't really decided yet. She didn't talk much at all about herself, but she seemed truly interested in what I had to say. All the time, I had it in my head to ask her to go to a movie with me; but, just as I'd worked it out in my mind and was ready to declare, the bus came. I would have to wait until Ancient History class the next day.

I watched the bus drive away until it turned the corner and disappeared. When I finally realized I was standing there at the bus stop alone, and that my toes were getting numb in my duck boots, it was almost dark. And, I still had the children's version of *Tom Sawyer* with me.

I didn't sleep much that night. Those eyes kept smiling at me. I even got up and wrote the note I would pass to her in class asking her to go to the movies with me that Saturday night.

Beatrice "Piggy" Levett taught Ancient History to my mother and my father. She was as old as the hills and a bitch on wheels. She spotted me passing the note up the row to Patricia and snatched it from her. The fat, old, beady-eyed, bowlegged sow read it out loud to the entire class; then made them all stay after school for laughing at me. The only thing that saved me from committing a rightful murder right then was catching Patricia's smiling eyes looking at me.

After our forced incarceration, I walked Patricia to the bus stop. David had already beaten it to Vic's and was waiting for me. Patricia told me that, even though she would love to go to the movies with me, her father didn't allow her to date yet. But, she did say she'd ask and that, if she could get permission, she'd meet me at the theater.

The next day was Saturday. The downtown Orpheum Theater had been there since the silent movie days and looked it. The modern age sometimes comes up against good old New England tradition and gets stopped in its tracks. The local dowagers on the historical society had, once again, pickled another monument to their own generation in the name of preservation. It still had the old wooden cordoned off box seats, that were now the reserved Saturday night passion pits, where the steady dating couples groped and out-petted each other for the full two hours. However, the fifteen cents my father had paid to get acquainted with my mother wasn't under the control of the historical society. I clutched the twenty dollar bill in my pocket, as I waited outside the theater on Saturday night. It didn't matter that it was one of the coldest nights of the winter and my nostrils were sticking together every time I breathed. Patricia was coming to meet me.

I wasn't surprised when David pulled up in his station wagon with two giggling gum-chewers from Vic's. But, I was surprised at his reaction at seeing me there. Usually, he would really get uptight if I hadn't told him about something I was going to do. Yet, he was his old bullshitting self and ready to party. He did a full, squealing U-turn and parked across the street. "See-ya inside," he chortled at me and hustled the two girls into the movie theater.

They were both dishwater blonds with too much makeup and attended All Saints Parish School for Girls up on the hill. Both of them had a reputation for putting out;

although, I don't think David had gotten to first base with either of them. But I could've cared less as I looked up both sides of the snow-banked street. Nothing but glowing streetlights and a few passing cars. I waited out under the theater marquee, my breath crystallizing in the raw cold, for half an hour more. Then, I went inside. Completely dejected.

The Orpheum passion pits were alive and well. David hissed to me from a back box. He was sitting between his two gum-snapping bookends with his arms draped around both of them. Margaret and Mary, I think their names were, but I really didn't give a shit at the time. I slipped into the box and sat next to one of David's escorts. The action flick on the screen didn't count. The surrounding heavy breathing and lip-smacking didn't count. Nothing counted. Patricia wasn't coming.

I vaguely remember David whispering in the girl's ear next to me and withdrawing his arm from around her. I'm not sure how long she'd been resting her head on my shoulder. I think it'd been quite awhile before her popping gum snapped me out of my deep fog.

I focused on the screen. Someone was lurking in the shadows of a darkened hallway. A person was approaching from the far end, looking for someone in the semidarkness. The music was building to an ominous climax. Our eyes met. It was Patricia looking right at me from the aisle. The gum-snapper was snuggled into the crook of my neck. The hurt in Patricia's eyes was caught in the flash of the fatal gunshot on the screen. A loud scream was followed by a dull thud. The scene on the screen went dark. I quickly shoved the girl away from me and looked frantically back toward the aisle. In that instant, Patricia had disappeared!

In a panic, I ran out of the theater after her, but it was dark, quiet, and bitter cold outside. All I could hear was my heart pumping. Patricia was nowhere in sight. Chilled to the bone, I walked the two miles back to my house and went to bed. I didn't even have her phone number.

Patricia and I didn't speak after that. I did make a weak attempt with my pencil trick, but it was no use. As David so aptly put it to me, "She's ancient history." *...the frog!...the frog!...*

David stood in front of the wall of dense trees and turned to me, like some Shakespearean actor, and exclaimed with a dramatic sweep of his hand, "This is a virgin forest!"

I looked at him from where I stood next to the station wagon and uttered, with some irritation, "So?"

He looked right at me and gestured toward the woods. "No one has ever set foot in there...except..."

"Except what?" I asked.

"I'll tell you later. Come on," David said and turned toward the woods. "Come on, Petey," he added.

I looked over at Petey. He had a funny look on his face, almost fearful. I called over to David, who had stepped just beyond the first row of trees. "What's going on?" I asked. "What's so great about going in there anyway?"

David stepped back out into the open. "Because, it's there and I'm not afraid to go in," he taunted, with the usual bravado he'd toss at me when I wouldn't do something he wanted me to do.

"What're you talking about?" I asked.

David's voice began to rise, "Hey, everyone up here is afraid to go into this forest."

I looked over at Petey who was looking at the ground and shifting his feet. "Come on," I scoffed at David.

"Oh?" he challenged. "You don't believe me? Watch." He looked at Petey with a shit-eating grin. "You comin', Petey?" he teased.

Petey glanced up at David. Again, I saw the flicker of fear in his beady eyes. He started picking at his scalp in earnest. "No," he finally muttered so low that I could hardly hear him.

David looked at me and said, quietly, "See what I mean?"

"So what?" I said, trying not to give ground.

David's eyes widened. He went into his leering act. "So...I'm going to be the first white man to find out about," he took a dramatic pause for the greatest effect, "...the mystery of the virgin forest!"

"Oh, God," I laughed, in spite of myself.

Then, David suddenly ran over to the station wagon and got out the two guns. He tossed the pistol to me. "Here, take this," he ordered with some urgency.

"What for? I asked apprehensively.

David was now into his 'high-charge.' "You must protect me from the evil that lurks deep within the forbidden forest," he pronounced. He then bounded back over the stone wall and headed toward the woods. He stopped at the edge of the forest and looked at me with a pirate's wide eye. "Come," he leered, "come-weeth-me."

I watched David turn and disappear among the

trees. Big Red beat it right after him. I looked over at Petey. He was staring at me. "Best not," he uttered ominously. I could almost smell the fear in him over the smell he gave off naturally. I hesitated and looked at the .22 pistol in my hand. Remembering that David hadn't loaded it, I thought it might be a good idea to catch up with him. Better David than Petey-the-weirdo.

I walked several yards into the forest. I couldn't remember having seen anything quite like it before. The tall pine trees were jammed right up close to each other. A kind of gray mossy growth hung from the lower branches like some sort of natural Christmas garland. What sun that managed to slip down in from above glittered off the dew that collected on the moss. I stopped and listened. It was so quiet all I could hear was a cricket chirping somewhere nearby and the sound of my own breathing. I started walking again. The sound of my own feet, crunching down on the thick carpet of century's old mulch beneath me, made me even more nervous than I already was. A lot of good an empty .22 pistol was going to do against whatever lived in there, I thought. I stopped again and called out, "Hey, David." No answer. "Cut it out, will you." I listened. Nothing. I walked on; then stopped next to a huge pine with long strands of gray, glittering moss reaching down to the ground. I started past the tree; then froze in a panic. I'm dead, I thought in that instant when I saw David standing next to the tree with his cheeks sucked in and his eyes bugging out at me. "Fuck!" I blurted out. "Goddamn you, David. Shit. Stop screwin' around."

"I got'cha-I got'cha," he laughed with glee and danced out in front of me.

Big Red charged back through the trees and happily

sniffed at my leg. Big Red always loved a good game. He sprayed his mark on the big mossy tree, to make sure that we would find our way back. I glared at David. "I'm going back to the car," I said.

"No-wait," he said quickly. "You have to help me find the answer. I'm a driven man."

"I don't care. I'm going back."

"Hey, come on, Billy-boy. Where's your adventurous spirit?"

"I left it in the car."

I started to turn back, then stopped and asked, "I thought we came up here to get laid and stuff. What're we doing walking around in the woods?"

David quickly stepped behind me, blocking my path back to the car. One of the more obvious techniques he'd pulled since we were little. "Okay-okay," he said, "I'll tell you the secret of the...virgin forest."

I rolled my eyes. "Oh, God," I groaned and tried to get around him.

David slapped his hand on my shoulder, holding his rifle down and away from me with his other hand. He became very serious and looked directly into my eyes. "You won't think it's so stupid when I tell you what it is," he said. "Sit over there," he ordered.

I looked over at the moss-covered fallen log he indicated and reluctantly sat on it. What choice did I have except to wait in the station wagon with old beady-eyes. "Okay, I'm all ears," I said sarcastically.

David set his rifle against the log and stepped back, as if he were about to begin a class lecture. I'd endured them many times before. I could get through another one. "Okay...look..." he began, "...have you noticed anything about these people up here?"

Here it comes I thought. "I've only seen three," I answered.

"Yeah, but, didn't you notice anything different about them?"

"Different from what?" I asked.

David prodded me, "Come on, Billy. Different from us."

I thought for a moment. Petey sure looked strange enough. The storekeeper wasn't what you'd call the demonstrative type. And then, there was Cyrus-the-zombie. "They sure don't talk much," I finally answered.

David heaved a resigned sigh. "Yeah-okay. You haven't had a chance to study them yet."

I stood up. I'd had it. "Where're you going?" David asked sharply.

"Back to the car."

"God," he said, "will you at least let me finish? You'll see what I mean at the dance tonight."

I looked right at David with some measure of defiance. "Yeah," I said. "Well, I would like to know what the hell you're talking about. You've been acting crazy ever since we got here."

David's eyes glowed with anticipation. They always did when he felt he'd scored a point. "I know," he breathed surreptitiously. "This place really turns me on... It's the end of the world."

I was getting bored with all of it. "Just tell me the big secret so we can go."

The old twinkle came into David's eyes. "Four-score-and-seven-years-ago..."

I turned away. "I'm leaving."

David stopped me. "Okay-okay, I'll tell you. Look, this little fishing town looks like a picture postcard, right?"

"Yeah-so?" I answered.

But, David was right. On the surface, the place did look like one of those pristine, rack-job postcards that you'd send someone to make them jealous they weren't along with you. If you took away the rabid dog by the road and weird Petey and the storekeeper and Cyrus-the-zombie, it would look like the perfect place to take a vacation or build a cottage like David's parents had done. In fact, I had noticed a couple of other cute little getaway places as we drove into town. I didn't see anyone in or around them, but it didn't matter. They wouldn't have had David's imagination along to spook them. I wasn't as fortunate. I mean, I don't want to give the wrong impression. David and I really did get along quite well most of the time. And, I have to admit that I enjoyed a lot of his bullshit, even if I didn't believe hardly any of it. Sometimes, I was even a little jealous that I wasn't able to pull off the kinds of elaborate stunts that he could. It was just, well, we were very different. David always ran ahead full blast and leaped over any giant chasm in his path without hesitation. Then, he'd land on the other side, look back at the abyss he'd just vaulted and say, "Jesus Christ, I didn't think I could do that!"

I, on the other hand, felt safer when I had everything in its place and knew what the hell was going on around me. Maybe, that's why I liked being with David, as opposed to being David. He made things exciting and at times - dangerous. I guess it was sort of the balance between us that made it work for so long. But, ever since Patricia, things seemed to change. I'd noticed a distance creeping into David - very subtle at first - but, there nonetheless. I'd asked him if anything was wrong, but he just blew me off; as he always did, when I'd bring up something that required some introspection on his part.

David paused, and then walked a few steps away, turning his back to me. "Well..." he began dramatically, "it is to most everyone who visits here, but underneath... it's a hell-hole of intrigue and debauchery."

"Come off it, will-ya. Geez."

David quickly turned to me. "I'm not kidding. Last summer I didn't have time to get all the facts, but this time I'm going to find out everything." He stopped. His voice lowered to almost a whisper, "I found out things that'll scare the crap out of you. Things that will..."

"What things?" I interrupted, hoping that it was just another one of David's high-charged stories. But, somehow, the feeling in my stomach told me that it might not be the case.

David spoke in measured tones, "There're only four last names in this whole town."

"So?"

"So there are almost two hundred people living here. That's so!"

That stopped me for a moment. I wasn't sure what this bit of statistical information was supposed to mean or how the hell it was supposed to affect me. I just knew it was affecting me.

David continued, "Which means, they're all married to each other. Which means, they're all interrelated and half crazy."

I thought about that for a minute. I remembered the town with the pointed heads and the black and white freaks in my dream. "So what?" I asked defensively.

"Look at Petey. He's got a long skinny jaw and kind of a flat head and a pointy nose and..."

I interrupted again. "Hey, David..."

His eyes shined as he went on excitedly, "The shopkeeper too. He looks the same as Petey and Cyrus the cripple. I saw a picture of him before he got all shot up and he looks just like Petey. And, wait'll we get to the dance. You'll see for yourself."

I studied David for a moment. My worst fear, with David, was that someday he might actually be telling the truth. "God, you're really hung up on this stuff," I told him.

"Yeah, I know. Come on." David picked up the rifle, turned and headed into the forest. Big Red sprayed another tree and lit out after him.

"Where're you going?" I called out.

"There's more. Come on," he shouted back through the trees. I hesitated. Once more, I was alone in David's virgin forest.

...It wasn't so much that I was always that annoyed at David. I guess I subconsciously knew that all his boasting and storytelling probably came from his having to constantly run for cover from his mother. I mean, I personally liked her. She was always very nice to me. When I was at David's house, she would normally encourage me to stay longer or to spend the night; which I usually did on Friday or Saturday or both, if nothing was going on at my house. That was usually the case, because my folks were pretty popular and most always got together with their friends on the weekends.

The fact that I didn't have any brothers or sisters didn't matter much to me; because I never really considered myself an only child. I was always with David. Also, his mother seemed to like having the two of us around a lot more, after David's older sister married a local cabinet maker; who I remembered used a shotgun full of birdshot to distress the wood he used to build reproductions of early American antiques. No one ever spoke about her after she moved out of her parent's house, and I don't remember seeing her around very much. It may have had something to do with her having to get married before graduating from high school. Pretty hush-hush, as I recall.

David's mother was forever plying me with all kinds of the sugary junk foods that she let David eat, trying to get me to tell her what her son was up to. I never finked, however. It was part of the bond that David and I had always had with each other. Nevertheless, it was a good thing I wasn't susceptible to zits like he was. She was constantly telling him to scrub his face, which certainly annoyed the hell out of David. She was always asking him why he couldn't be more like me and throwing it up to him that he wouldn't have had to repeat the fourth grade, if he'd studied hard like I did. I could tell he resented her a lot when she'd pull that. He'd go into one of his black moods and do his mean-spirited imitations of her out of earshot.

One day, she found a condom in his wallet and the shit really hit the fan. We all had the little 'circle-of-manhood' showing through our leather wallets to impress the girls, and each other. The only difference was, my mom never went through my things or - if she had - she never told me about it. She must have figured that carrying around the same rubber for a year was pretty harmless stuff. Not so with David's mother. She twisted his ear right in front of me and jerked him into the pantry and slammed the door, leaving me in the kitchen alone. All I heard was her screaming at him and boxing his ears and David whimpering, "I'm sorry, Ma. I won't do it again. Please, Ma. I'm sorry."

When these tirades were over, she'd call Reverend Stevens the Pastor at our Congregational Church and invite him over to have a 'talk' with David about his 'responsibilities.' The good Reverend would drop everything and come right away. The discounted heating oil for the church was at stake.

It always surprised me when she'd lay into David like that. She seemed so benign and pleasant otherwise, sort of plain and plump, like a lot of New England mothers, with lots of dimples. Dimpled elbows. Dimpled knees - front and back. Dimpled chin and cheeks. And kind of a dimple for a mouth that she'd purse whenever she didn't get her way, which was most of the time. Through it all, though, David had become quite deft at sidestepping his mother's little puritan games...

I looked back in the direction toward where Petey would be waiting at the station wagon and decided to follow David and Big Red deeper into the woods. David's trail and Big Red's markers lead me through the dense forest, for a mile or so. I didn't bother to call out after them; I knew that would've just given David another opportunity to scare the crap out of me.

The trees finally thinned and I could hear the ocean

just up ahead of me. As I slowly emerged from the woods, I saw David standing at the edge of a high jagged cliff a few yards away. Big Red ran over and sniffed excitedly, then trotted back to the edge of the cliff.

"Here we are!" David proclaimed to the world.

I walked up beside David and looked down at the sheer, almost perpendicular cliff that dropped down to a small, isolated strip of rock and driftwood studded beach below.

"Here we are, what?" I asked. My sarcasm was still intact.

David's voice became hushed. "This is...the secret," he uttered.

"It's the ocean. Big deal."

"Yeah, it's the ocean. But, it's also where this little fishing village hides the truth."

I looked at David. "You've really flipped out, you know that?"

"Oh, really? Then, tell me what happens to people when they marry their first cousins and knock up their sisters."

"I dunno, what?"

"Come on," he asked, "what happens to the babies?"

I thought for a moment. There was something in David's voice. "I...I guess they're retarded or something."

"Right! Because, the blood's too close and they can be born mongos and deformed and all weirded out."

I looked down at the ocean and the little beach below us. "What's that got to do with being out here?" I asked, not that sure I really wanted to know.

David became overly solemn and stared down at

the waves lapping up on the solitary strip of white sand. "This...is where they put them..." he said in an appropriate hush.

"What?" I asked incredulously.

As if to firmly emphasize his point, David turned and faced me. "This is where they throw away the deformed babies," he said.

I stood there looking at him. Even Big Red stopped running all around and was looking curiously over the edge of the cliff at the beach below.

"Right-down-there..." David whispered.

"I don't believe you."

"Sometimes, the tide washes away the sand and you can see little white bones sticking up."

"Who told you that?"

"Petey," David said flatly.

"Now, I know you've flipped."

David looked at me and said evenly, "His cousin...is his...mother."

"God, will you stop. He's just a dumb hick who probably has nothing better to do than tell stupid stories." I was really getting exasperated.

David just gave me his challenging grin. "Let's go down there then," he said.

"Are you kidding? I'm going back."

"Then, you believe him, don't you."

"I do not. I'm just going back, that's all."

I turned and started for the trees. David quickly stepped in front of me, cutting me off. "You believe him or you'd go down there with me."

"Will you stop screwin' around, this is dumb."

"No adventurous spirit."

"That's right. Let's go back."

David just grinned at me. "Okay, Billy-boy," he said sarcastically, "but, you'll never know the real truth about the secret of the virgin forest."

"Oh, geez." I brushed by David and walked back into the woods. I didn't look back to see if David was coming. I didn't have to. I could hear him walking a distance behind me and Big Red running to catch up.

I guess we were about halfway back when David finally broke his silence. "Go ahead," he shouted dramatically from the woods behind me. "Go through life not experiencing anything." Then he hit me with, "Remember our bond?" I just kept walking. "I'm telling the truth, Billy, and you don't believe me."*...the frog!...the frog!...*

"Believing you or some moron's stupid story is different," I shouted back over my shoulder and kept walking through the thick undergrowth.

David was always screwing around, so none of his theatrics surprised me in the least. Not even his far-out story about dropping deformed babies off a cliff in a 'virgin forest.' But, something seemed a little different. We'd driven over three hundred and eighty miles on David's promise that this was - "the land of endless pussy." However, in only a matter of a few hours, it seemed more like "the land of the living dead." And, David wasn't letting up as he usually did after he tripped out on his imagination.

We came to the fallen log where David had made me sit and listen to him. Big Red quickly spritzed the log. David caught up and clapped me on the shoulder, turning me around to face him. "But, what if it's true, Billy? You can't go around closing your mind off to everything."

"My mind isn't closed. This is just dumb and none of our business." I turned and jumped over Big Red's marked log and continued on through the woods.

"It's not dumb," David shouted from behind me. "I told you this was the end of the world. These people live by a different code. They have their own way of doing things."

I stopped and turned around. I could see David through the trees, still standing on the other side of the log. Big Red stopped, too. "Like throwing babies off a cliff?" I challenged.

"Yeah!" David shot back defensively.

We both stood our ground, several yards apart through the mossy trees. David was still standing on the other side of the log. "Okay," I shouted, "if you're so smart what about the law?"

David waited a moment; then he answered matter-of-factly, "What law?"

"The police. If it's true, the police would..."

David quickly jumped up on the log and interrupted me. "There's no police up here," he announced seriously. "I told you, they take care of things themselves. They have their own law."

I hesitated for a moment. As much as I wanted to chalk this up as just another one of David's exploding mind games, the squeamish feeling in my stomach told me something different. "Jesus," I finally uttered, "you're really talking crazy, ya-know?" I looked through the trees at David standing up on the fallen log. Somehow, he seemed much bigger and taller than he had just a few moments before. "You're changing or something," I said.

David jumped down from the log and ran toward me through the trees. "No, I'm not," he shouted enthusiastically. "It's just that everything is so alive to me now." He charged right up to me, almost nose to nose, his eyes sparkling with excitement. "I want to know everything about everything!"

He backed off as if I was supposed to be caught up in his euphoria. I wasn't. "How dramatic," I responded with my patented cynical defense. Then I asked, "Look, do you mind if I don't happen to believe all of this crap?"

David feigned innocence. Another talent he had. "Hey, don't let me stop you."

I heaved a sigh and walked on through the trees. David didn't say anything more, but I could feel his eyes following me. I also knew the look on his face. The same look he always got when he didn't win. Pissed!

The rest of the day was pretty quiet. Only because I didn't feel like talking to David about the mating habits of the local inbreds, and his friend Petey wasn't what one would call a brilliant conversationalist, nor someone I'd intended to create any kind of extended relationship with. They had a few beers in the living room and found an old checker game to occupy themselves. I took another nap in the bedroom with Big Red curled up at my feet, snoozing off his first venture into the 'virgin forest.'

SEVEN

THE SKUNK RUN

...The darkness that wrapped around me was stifling. I couldn't get my breath. The silhouette of a black-and-white monster was standing over me surrounded by a blinding oblong light. If I tried to run, the monster would call the others and slaughter me right there. I might already be dead. I tried to scream, but my cries caught in my throat. The monster reached out and grabbed my foot..."Wake up!"...it shouted from a great distance. I tried to free myself, but its grip tightened and wouldn't let go. "Wake up, Billy!" it shouted again. This time much closer. I jerked my leg free with all my strength and sat bolt upright. Suddenly, a blinding light filled my brain. I looked straight into the wild eyes of the horrible monster standing in the doorway with its hand on the bedroom light switch...

"What's the matter with you? You dreamin' or somethin'?" David asked. "Come on, it's getting dark. It's time to go." I watched David turn and leave the bedroom. Big Red jumped off the foot of my bed, where he'd been sleeping, and followed David. I was fully awake and my heart was slowing to its normal rhythm. The monster had disappeared.

It was an especially dark night. No moon yet, and

no downtown glow from all the streetlights back home. The station wagon's headlights sliced through the inky blackness like two white knives, as David maneuvered along a twisting back road. Suddenly, a huge eight point buck stood frozen right in our path. Its eyes caught like two terrified glowing coals. David jammed on the brakes and slid to a stop, just a few feet from the frightened animal. "Jesus Christ," I uttered. The first words I'd spoken since that afternoon. Big Red barked furiously from the rear of the station wagon and the buck leaped off into the darkness. David continued on for several hundred yards; then whipped a right turn onto a rutted road.

I was stubbornly trying my best not to let anything else get to me, but curiosity and an innate fear of the unknown can do wonders at helping to break one's self-imposed silence. "What the hell's a skunk run?" I finally asked.

"Quiet," David hushed. "We're almost there."

I was getting used to Petey's stink and looked around at him sitting in the back seat. He wasn't much help. Just grinned at me with his yellow teeth and picked his stubbled hair.

David slowed, as he drove through the entrance to a town dump spread out in a large clearing in the middle of some woods. He stopped and doused the headlights, but kept the motor running. I could just make out David's silhouette in the darkness. "Okay, Billy, you drive," he whispered.

"What for?" I whispered back.

David leaned closer to me in the darkness. "Petey and me are gonna ride on the front fenders. The choice part of the dump is right up ahead. I want'cha to drive real slow, and when I give you the signal, stop and put the lights on quick. And, don't let Big Red out of the car."

David reached under the front seat and slid out the .22 rifle and the pistol. He handed the pistol to Petey; then they quietly got out of the station wagon and eased the doors shut. I could barely see them, as they silently crawled up onto the front fenders. "Forward ho," David rasped.

I inched the station wagon forward in the darkness. Two large black mounds of trash rose up in front of us, silhouetted against the night sky. David silently waved me closer and then held up his hand to stop. I cut the engine and waited in the quiet with my hand on the headlight switch. No one moved. Not even Big Red in the back of the station wagon. Then, David gave me a signal. I pulled the light switch. The headlights blasted on, illuminating the huge trash heaps in front of us. Little dark things stopped and looked into the bright lights. Startled. Their little beady eyes sparkled with fear.

"There's one!" David shouted and leaped off the car. He ran right at a mound of trash, firing his .22 rifle as he waded into the refuse. The crack of shots ricocheted through the trees.

Petey fired at the top of the other mound and ran toward it. Big Red barked furiously at them. David charged up to the top of the trash mound and emptied his rifle into a large cardboard box. Petey got off two more quick shots into the darkness; then stopped firing. I could see David standing over the cardboard box, sweat streaming down his face. "Hey, Billy," he shouted to me, "bring the flashlight. It's in the glove compartment."

Petey ran over to David, as I fumbled for the

flashlight. "Get yo'ahs?" he asked David.

"I think so."

"Missed mine," Petey said without any emotion.

I waded through the trash up to David and handed him the flashlight. David gingerly tilted the edge of the cardboard box with the tip of his rifle and shined the flashlight inside. A look of complete satisfaction came over his face. "Got'im," he uttered triumphantly.

"Yep," Petey agreed.

I didn't say anything. I just stared down at the bloody mess inside the box.

David announced, "The great white hunter strikes again!" Then he thumped his chest and trumpeted a shrill Tarzan yell. Petey grinned stupidly and gurgled a laugh. "Time for a beer," David declared and marched victoriously down through the trash, back toward the station wagon. Petey followed right on his heels - the obedient little soldier. I lingered for a moment, staring down at the pathetic little black animal with its red blood splattered on its pure white stripe. A lump began to swell in my throat... *the frog!...the frog!...*

A sudden snap of a twig to my left startled me out of my catalepsy. I turned and peered into the darkness. Nothing. Then, a crunch. Something stepping on dry leaves. I turned again, trying to see beyond the glow of the headlights. David blasted the car horn and scared the shit out of me. I sensed something moving very close to me and looked in the other direction. My entire body reacted at once. I whirled and looked right into the glowing red eyes of the diseased creature-from-hell that had greeted us upon our arrival in postcard town. The shock immobilized me. Lethal white foam dripped slowly from its yellow fangs. The demon dog lowered its head and let out a low gurgling growl. I stood stalk-still, not daring to flinch or blink. Sensing my fear, the rabid animal started inching its quivering body forward. Its red eyes glued to mine. I had to make a move or die. David made it for me. He blasted the car horn again. Both the dog and I recoiled at the same time. Before I could think about it, I bounded off the trash heap in three giant leaps and sprinted for the station wagon.

"What the hell were you doin' up there?" David asked as I jumped into the car and slammed the door tight.

"Talking to an old friend," I mumbled, trying to catch my breath and not wishing to relive the experience.

We'd driven about a mile back toward the cottage before I realized that Petey was sitting in the front seat between David and me. I guess the shock of seeing old Fido was still on my face, because Petey was staring at me. I forced a grin and looked out my window at the passing darkness.

"Well, ma-man," David finally asked me, "what'd you think of your first skunk run?"

"...S'okay."

"It's your turn tomorrow night," David announced, then waited for my reaction. I didn't react, so he dropped into his dramatic mode. "You still owe me a kill," he said.

"What?" I uttered with a twinge.

"Our sacrifice!"

I just looked at him, barely able to make out his features as we drove along the dark wooded road.

"The frog, remember? You never made a living sacrifice for...the bond."

I was stunned. "God, that was four years ago."

"Right, but I never forget a sacrifice," David said, then looked over Petey at me. I guess he could see my perplexed expression, because he began to laugh wickedly. "Petey, get us a beer," he ordered, still laughing.

Petey scootched around between us and reached into the cooler full of beer on the back seat. Big Red growled from way in the back compartment. I looked around, as Petey came up with three beers and opened them. Big Red was cowering up against the rear hatch, as if he was trying to get away from something. Petey passed out the beers. "Ahhhhhh," David gushed, after he took a long swill, "relief for the thirsty hunter."

Big Red started to whimper loudly from the back. "What's wrong with him?" I asked and looked around.

David looked in the rearview mirror. "I dunno. Quiet, Big Red."

Big Red scrunched himself up tighter in the corner and let out a long, mournful howl. "Something's wrong with..." Then, it hit me right square in my nostrils. "Jesus, what's that smell?"

"What sme..." It hit David, too. "Oh, shit!" he exclaimed. It didn't hit Petey. Any sense of smell that he had was smothered by his own stench. David hit the gas and we roared off into the night, back toward the town.

All three of us hit our heads on the roof of the car, as the station wagon leaped the ridge and raced down through the village. Except for a few lonely streetlights and a stray cat, the place looked empty. Then, holding my nose pinched hard between my fingers, I caught a glimpse of the grotesque figure of Cyrus Peak standing in the semi-darkness between two buildings, watching us go by, as he held a bottle of whisky up to his mouth-hole.

Back at the cottage, David and I frantically ripped off all of our clothing outside on the driveway. David ran naked to a small storage shed next to the cottage, found a shovel, and hurriedly started digging a hole. I snapped on the outside floodlights, ran into the kitchen bare-assed, and ransacked the cupboards for some vinegar. Once, when we were little, David and I had been sprayed by a skunk that Big Red had flushed from its burrow. My mother used one of my grandmother's cure-alls and washed our hides with distilled vinegar to get the stink out of our skin. No vinegar. I ran back outside. David was digging like crazy next to our pile of skunk-spritzed clothes. Big Red was frantically rolling around in the dirt. Petey was leaning against a tree in the shadows, staring at David. I noticed that there was a strange, fascinated look on his face as he watched David digging the hole without any clothes on. Then, Petey looked over at me and I realized I was naked, too. My hands automatically covered my privates. "I can't find the vinegar," I shouted at David.

"It's under the goddamned sink. Hurry up and take a shower."

I glanced at Petey. He was still staring at me. I turned and ran back into the cottage.

"Fucking skunk!" I heard David shout angrily. Like the poor skunk had any say in the matter.

I rummaged around under the sink for the vinegar. "Hey, Petey," David said, loud enough for me to hear in the kitchen, "gimme your clothes. I'll bury'em an' you can have some of mine."

"Nah, I'll go up home. See'ya at the bahn dance,"

Petey answered in a monotone. The little rodent probably couldn't tell the skunk smell from his own B.O., I thought, as I found the bottle of white vinegar and raced for the shower.

Whoever passed down the fact that vinegar could cut the power of skunk spray must have been a genius in his time because it worked. After I had completely washed my violated body in it, then scrubbed myself raw with a shower brush and soap, I actually couldn't smell it anymore.

When I was little, I remember my grandfather - on my mother's side - calling it ‘nature's perfume’ every time we'd smell a skunk's scent somewhere. I'm not so sure I agreed with him; but the memory soothed me some as I turned my face up into the shower, letting it blast down over me.

Finally, after one of the most bizarre days I'd ever spent, I began to relax and let my mind wander... *Patricia...* Did she ever think of me after that terrible night at the Orpheum? Maybe, I should have tried harder to explain to her that I wasn't with another girl. I knew what she must have gone through to convince her father to allow her to go to a movie with me and then see me sitting in the passion pit... Shit... SHIT! The shock of having a full glass of ice water dumped over the shower door onto you, while you're daydreaming under the hot water, can damn near give you a heart attack.

I jerked back hard against the tiled wall and saw David's shadow through the frosted shower door. "Goddamn you David!" I shouted.

David's head appeared up over the glass door and he leered down at me, "Man, look at that dick," he said in mock surprise. "What a fuckin' wanger."

I tried to fling water at him. "Screw you."

"Please. Oh, pleeeeth," he lisped.

"Fruit."

"How did you know?" David grinned, batting his eyes at me.

I couldn't help laughing. David could usually pull the most outrageous prank on me and I'd usually end up going along with it. Maybe, it was because he could make me feel there was no malice or underlying reason for what he did. Anyway, I laughed along with him. "Get outta here," I said.

"Don't use all the hot water."

"I'm almost done."

"J'a use the vinegar?"

"Yeah," I answered and put my face up into the shower spray again, "it stings like hell."

I had my eyes shut tight. I shouldn't have. The shock of the second glass of ice water hitting by back was stronger than the first. "You-son-of-a-bitch!" I screamed and charged out of the shower after David, who was already beating it out of the bathroom.

I grabbed a towel from the towel rack and quickly twirled a snap-towel as I chased David through the kitchen. He darted into the bedroom and slammed the door in my face. David tried to hold the door shut on me, as I shoved against it with all my might; but he was too weak from laughing so hard to hold me back. I leaped at the door with my bare foot and kicked it open. David flew back onto his bed and tried to shield himself with his pillow against my snap-towel attack.

"Hey, don't," David laughed, loving the game. I

snapped the towel and got him right on his bare ass. "Ow!" he yelled. "Come on, cut it out."

I whipped the towel around again and snapped him on his leg. "Say you're sorry," I ordered. This time, I was in control of the situation - maybe for the first time in our lives. It felt good. I twirled the towel and snapped it hard, getting off another direct hit.

"Shit!" he yelped and leaped off the bed. "Come on, stop, will-ya." Amazingly, David was still laughing as I snapped and missed.

"Say you're sorry you threw water on me," I shouted. David tried to beat it out the door. I was too fast and blocked his way. Slowly, I twirled the towel and advanced on my prey, forcing him back into a corner, making him cower and grovel for his life.

David pleaded with me, and clapped his hands over his sensitive targets, protecting himself against an imminent snap. "Okay-okay-I'm-sorry-I-threw-water-on-you."

I made one more threat with the snap-towel then backed off and let the defeated enemy go. I'd won and had shown compassion toward the vanquished. We both collapsed onto our beds with laughter.

"Bastard," David said, getting his breath back. "Gimme the towel, I gotta get cleaned up."

I tossed him the towel and rolled over on my bed, inadvertently exposing my ass. In the same instant that the thought hit me, so did the pain of the well-aimed snap on the fleshy part of my butt. "Sucker!" David shouted gleefully and scampered out of the bedroom, laughing all the way.

"You prick," I yelled after him, mad as hell at

myself for getting aced.

I was already to go after David, but Big Red ran in and jumped up on the bed next to me. He started licking my face, as he always did when he knew I was distressed. I instinctively put my arm around his thick red neck and nuzzled him affectionately. A ritual that we'd gone through since the little Irish setter had become part of our lives.

Even though he was technically David's dog, it was apparent that Big Red felt just as comfortable at my house as he did at David's. My father even installed a doggie-door in the back pantry entrance where food and water were always available for him. And, since our house was just a long street away from Big Red's, it was just a matter of where he wished to spend the night. Big Red always seemed to show up when I was feeling bad and had a way of helping put things in perspective for me. That's why I loved him so much.

There were no lasting psychological effects from my leaving myself open for a counterattack in the towel fight. Given David's calculating mind, I should have expected it. So, we got it together and went about getting ourselves ready to head out for the local barn dance, as if nothing had happened. It was our usual way of putting an end to a tense situation.

David was already outside. I was putting the finishing touches on my hair. An attribute that I definitely held over David, since I had very straight, dark hair and I could give it a rakish flip. David had curly, auburn hair that his mother made him keep very short. She was afraid he'd get head lice. Although, I definitely wasn't the forward type, I could tell that some girls liked the way I combed my hair; so I ignored David's slams about my 'mousse-curl' and worked to perfect the effect in the bathroom before we left for the dance. One never knew, even on this forgotten planet, there just might be one girl who was miraculously bypassed by the local gene pool.

...Maybe someone like Patricia. However, I didn't hold out much hope. Also, to me, there wasn't anyone else quite like Patricia. My heart still hadn't gotten over her...

EIGHT

BARN DANCE

David hit the horn impatiently, as I locked Big Red in the cottage for the evening. This time, he wasn't going to con his way into going along with us. Besides, he still had the residual fragrance of 'nature's perfume' on him. Even his forlorn look through the living room window didn't help his cause. He'd just have to wait it out. David blasted the horn again. "Hurry up," he shouted, as I crossed the drive to the station wagon and got in. "God, you're worse than a girl. Did you get every hair in place, sweetie?" David scoffed.

"I couldn't find the pit juice."

David reached over and popped the glove compartment open. He grabbed a spray can of deodorant and flipped it to me. "Hey, we don't wanna chance drivin' away the local talent," he chided.

I grabbed the deodorant and sprayed my pits up under my shirt. "If they're related to Petey, I don't think they'll be offended."

David gunned the station wagon in a circle and roared away into the darkness. "Yeee-haaa!" he whooped, as I looked back at the cottage. I could see Big Red's silhouette in the small calico curtained window.

David wheeled the car along a dark, forest-lined back road. I sprayed some more deodorant up under my arms. "Are you sure you can't smell the vinegar? I know I smell like a salad."

"Open a couple of beers. We gotta get a glow on before we get there."

The station wagon sped over the forest road, as a bright moon began to rise above the trees. I snapped open two cans of beer and handed one to David, as we raced through the night.

A faded red barn sat away from the road in the middle of the surrounding forest. Two large floodlights, wired to a tall pine, illuminated the rutted, dirt parking lot in front. Most of the vehicles that haphazardly filled the area were battered pickups; some of which might have been worth a fortune on the vintage car market. But, who the hell knew the town existed besides David and me and a few clueless vacationers, who probably built their getaway cabins on a whim and never returned. To this day, I can't recall ever seeing the place on any road map. Certainly, not one put out by the Maine tourist bureau.

As David drove in and looked for a place to park, I noticed three men standing beneath one of the floodlights passing a bottle among themselves. They had the same gaunt, haunted look that Petey had. David drove the station wagon aggressively into an opening across from them, next to the trees. Their pin-hole eyes darted in our direction. They weren't talking to each other, just quietly passing the bottle of booze around and looking suspiciously at us. It gave me the creeps and we'd only just arrived. "This is it," David announced and gulped the rest of his beer.

"Not much going on," I uttered, a little unnerved

by the group of locals staring at us.

"Just wait," David said, as he got out of the car and surveyed the territory. Then, he leaned in and instructed me in hushed authoritative tones, "Okay, now listen to me for a minute. The girls up here are a little different than back home, so," he underscored this, "follow my lead."

"Hey, I'm not some dummy ya-know."

"Shhh," David uttered forcefully. He glanced over at the three creepy guys drinking under the floodlight, who were all staring our way. I wondered if they had three out of the four names in the town. David looked back at me with his exaggerated warning look. "Yeah, you're a big time city boy. But, this is a very different place."

I looked around at the local townies. "You can say that again."

"Let's find Petey," David ordered.

We slipped through the passel of jammed together junkers and pickup trucks and headed for the entrance to the old barn, a small opened door next to the padlocked main barn doors. David leaped up the three rickety steps and was inside ahead of me, as usual.

I started up the stairs after him and stopped. Something to my left caught my eye, something moving just within the shadows of the trees that ringed the parking lot and the barn. I stepped down off the stairs and gazed into the semi-darkness. It was Cyrus Peak the cripple standing there, almost hidden behind a tree. I don't know why, but I stood where I was and watched him for a moment. He was fumbling with a pint of whiskey with his shaking hands, trying to unscrew the top. The unopened bottle dropped to the ground. Cyrus tried to bend over to pick it up. From where I was standing, I could see that the machine gun bullets that had ripped through his body must have frozen his spine. He could only bend low enough to keep the bottle just out of reach. The effort strained him and he slowly pulled back up. Our eyes met. I could feel my face redden. I looked away and started back up the steps. I stopped on the landing in front of the entrance to the barn and looked back at Cyrus. He was bent over again, trying in vain to retrieve his bottle. I reasoned that he must have been in great pain and needed his sedative to relieve it. Without thinking any further, I jumped down from the landing and quietly walked over to within a few feet of Cyrus, trying to avoid looking at his horribly scarred face. His disfigured head jerked up from his bent over position, startled at my being there. I picked up the whiskey bottle and unscrewed the top. As I handed him the bottle, which he quickly clutched in his trembling, bone-thin hands, I couldn't help looking at him. He didn't speak. I wasn't sure if he even could. He just stared at me for a long moment with his one good scar-tissued eye, then turned and shuffled away into the quiet darkness of the woods. I stood there for a moment more. There was something... something in his fixed, unemotional expression. And, there was that smell. I didn't recognize it at first, and then it hit me. It was the odor of the same cheap men's cologne that David and I first used in junior high school, thinking that it would attract the girls. It didn't. I turned back and hurried into the barn.

The small entrance door led into a dingy little, dimly-lit anteroom, just off the main barn where the dance was going on. A bare bulb hung by a frayed wire from an overhead loft beam, illuminating the chipping whitewash that had been slapped on the walls by one of the local artisans to cover up the fact that the room was formerly a horse stall. The musty smell gave it away, along with the fact that my sinus cavities immediately began to fill up. I was somewhat allergic to horsehair. David came hurrying out of the main 'ballroom' to get me.

"Where the hell have you been? I turned around and you were gone."

"I had to take a leak."

"Come on," David commanded and led the way to the open door to the main room; where a bent and bony middle-aged woman with grayish-yellow hair and sallow skin sat slumped at a scarred wooden table taking money and stamping hands with a rubber ink stamp.

"Give'er two bucks," David ordered.

The woman eyed me suspiciously through tiny, wrinkled eyes. She had the deeply lined, squinched-up mouth of someone who'd lost all of her teeth. Little knobby growths with black hairs growing out of them dotted her narrow protruding chin. Petey's sister's cousin on his brother's mother's side, I thought, as I dug the two dollars out of my jeans and paid her. She banged the rubber stamp down on a small ink pad and stamped my hand extra hard with a black X. I guess she didn't like the fact that David and I had different last names than the four she was familiar with. However, I was getting used to the fact that we weren't socially acceptable and was more than willing to live with it without any guilt. David led me inside the main room.

Although, I'd never been to a barn dance quite like it before; with all that had already happened since we'd arrived, I wasn't the least bit surprised at what it looked like. The old, abandoned barn had been crudely converted into a place for square dancing. A two-foot high wooden platform, against the far wall, held a local five piece band - of sorts. Fiddle player, accordion, guitar, base and drummer. I was also sure they were proficient on the jew's harp. If this wasn't twanger country, nothing was.

A scroungy old square dance caller stepped to the vintage Electro-Voice microphone and called to the thirty or so attendees, scattered around the dimly lighted catacomb, to form up in the center for another go around. Several somber looking couples paired up in groups under strings of dusty, paper lantern covered lightbulbs that crisscrossed above their heads. Torn, faded crepe paper streamers hung in limp loops from the dark board walls. Nice touch, I thought.

The old dance caller began twanging his raspy, rapid-fire commands, "Awright, sistahs'n'bruthas." ...Right on that one... "Gatha'roun' an' swing-ya-pahtnah-up'n'down. Do-si-do-an'a'roun'yah-go." The caller continued and the dancers shuffled into their automatic routines, like rusting robots from out of the past. No wonder Paul Revere thought he was better off hanging around the Boston area.

I leaned into David and spoke so none of the locals could hear me, "Hey, I can't dance this stuff."

"So, what," he said. Then lowered his voice to an excited whisper, "See what I mean about these people?"

I looked at them. "What?" I asked.

"The people," David insisted, "look at them. They all look the same. Fuckin' mouth-breathers."

"What?" I said again, looking at the groups of squared-off, ragtag dancers as they shuffled listlessly through the steps the caller fed them through the scratchy portable loud speaker.

"Never mind," David said, getting increasingly exasperated with me. "Come on, there's Petey."

I followed David through the zombie-like dancers over to a far corner under an old hay loft. Petey was alone in the shadows, leaning against a support beam, staring blankly at the dance floor. It was the first time that I'd noticed that Petey's mouth hung slightly open, like there wasn't enough muscle in his thin lower lip to close it. Or, maybe, no one ever taught him how to.

"Hey, Petey," David said brightly. Petey 'the tour guide' didn't answer. Just gave me a long once-over with his little thumbtack eyes, as he reached into his filthy, threadbare jacket and produced a full bottle of 150 proof backwoods hooch. He glanced around furtively and then handed the bottle to David.

"This the good stuff?" David asked, his eyes sparkling. Petey nodded.

David showed me the corked bottle of crystal clear whiskey. "This'll tear your goddamned head off." Then, he turned his back on the dancers and uncorked the bottle. "Here goes nothin'," he declared and gave me his daredevil wink as he filled his mouth and gulped it straight down. David reacted as if a red-hot poker had suddenly been shoved down his throat. His face went ashen. "Jesus-God," he rasped wide-eyed. Petey grinned his green-toothed grin. David sucked in some air and wiped his burning lips on his sleeve. "Shit," he coughed and handed the bottle to me.

"Pass," I said.

"You've got to," David gagged. "It's great."

I looked at the bottle of poison apprehensively.

David was getting his voice back. "Come on, don't be a candy-ass. They feed this to their babies up here." ...And, throw them off the cliff when they explode... I thought to myself.

Very carefully, I tipped the bottle to my lips, hoping they wouldn't peel off. I took a very slight pull of the rancid stuff and instantly gasped out loud, as the revolting liquid seared my throat like molten lava racing down an active volcano. I tried to spit it out, but I wasn't quick enough. It was already eating holes in my stomach lining.

Suddenly, as I fought off a vomit attack, a tall grizzled, gray-faced man in faded denim overalls appeared out of nowhere. He ripped the bottle right out of my hands. "Do yo'ah drinkin' outside," he spit through brown tobacco chew-juice that ran into the creases at the edge of his thin, turned-down mouth.

I was too startled and reeling from the firewater to say anything. David just stared at him, not knowing what to do next. Petey turned and started walking away. "Come on," he twanged dully to both of us. Without saying a word, David and I followed Petey toward the exit.

As Petey and David walked out of the barn dance into the little anteroom, I glanced back through the dancers at the grizzled man. He had the hooch bottle tipped straight up and was gulping the rotgut as if he were quenching his thirst with a Coke.

Out in the reception stall, several people were coming in, including two teenaged girls who David was already pinning. The scrawny, anorexic one wouldn't have drawn the attention of the dead skunk or the demon dog. She had stringy, dishwater blond hair that hung limply around a bony, haunted face. I couldn't tell if there was anything going for her under the faded wash'n'wear dress and the snagged buttoned sweater she had on, because she had her skinny arms crossed tightly around her chest. Definitely cut from the local gene pool. However, the girl with her didn't seem half bad. No Patricia, mind you, but she had shiny dark hair and a clear tawny complexion, certainly acceptable for this neck of the woods. Actually, she looked kind of out of place. My guess was that she must've been visiting like we were. I was wrong. David whispered excitedly in my ear, "Jesus, there she is."

"Who?" I whispered back.

"The girl I told you about. Look at those tits."

I looked. She did have quite large breasts that stood straight out under the white, low-cut peasant blouse she was wearing with a simple cinch-belted A-lined skirt, white turned down sox, and polished penny loafers out of another era.

I watched her pay the toothless lady, who gave her a red-gummed grin as she lightly stamped her hand. There seemed to be a certain softness and seductive sexiness about the girl that belied her heritage. Also, unlike her friend's, her mouth was closed. She looked our way, brightened, and walked toward us with her gape-mouthed friend close behind.

"Hey, Petey," she said with an easy smile and a glance in David's and my direction, "what're you doin'?"

"Nothin'," Petey mumbled. "Wanna drink?"

"Maybe later," she answered and looked right at David and me with a twinkle in her large brown eyes. "Who're your friends?"

Ever the opportunist, David answered too quickly,

"I'm David from the summer house up the road from town, an' this is my friend, Billy."

I nodded, which was all I could come up with at the moment. Actually, if David hadn't made his move, we'd probably still be standing there while I figured out what to say. It'd taken me two weeks to work up the courage to ask Patricia out and then I had to use my stupid pencil trick.

"Hi," she said coyly, "just visitin'?"

I started to brave an answer, but David was on a roll. "Yeah. We're usin' my folk's place for a few days."

"I'm Sandy and this's Mildred," she offered with a smile, indicating her emaciated friend who was hiding behind her.

"I remember you from last year," David rushed. "Sure you won't come outside for a drink?"

Sandy cocked her head. Her eyes seemed to brighten at the invitation. "Maybe, we'll see you later. I gotta do some dancin' first."

"Yeah-right. We'll be outside," David said enthusiastically.

Sandy smiled knowingly, turned and took her timid friend, Mildred, firmly by the hand. "Come on, Mildred," she said, like a mother to a child, and led her toward the door to the barn dance.

David had 'conquest' written all over his face. "Whoa!" he uttered jubilantly under his breath, then ordered Petey and me outside. "Come on, I gotta get some fuel for my jet engine."

As David headed out, with Petey following, I hesitated and watched after Sandy and Mildred. Sandy stopped at the doorway and glanced back at me with a little coquettish smile. I cursed myself for not having enough control to stop my face from getting red. Then, before I could smile back, she disappeared into the barn. I stood there a moment more, in the middle of the whitewashed room, until the blood in my cheeks subsided. I caught the toothless lady staring at me with a dark, disapproving look and went outside to join David and Petey.

From where I stood on the small landing just outside the door, I didn't see David and Petey anywhere. I looked to my left over the jammed together trucks and junkers. The local three-man social club was still gathered under the flood lights drinking it up. But, one of them was standing apart from the other two and staring across the parking lot right at me. Although he was too far away for me to see what he looked like; he was definitely taller than his friends and, silhouetted against the floodlight, seemed rather menacing.

"Psst. Over here," David whispered from the semi-darkness beside the barn, just to my right. I jumped down off the landing and hurried into the shadows. David was watching Petey take another bottle of white lightning out of a small crevice in the glacier rock foundation that held up the old barn. Petey uncorked the full bottle and took a gulp without flinching; then passed it to David whose eyes were gleaming at me. "Did I lie? Huh? Did you see those fuckin' boobs? They're gigantic. Did'ja see'im?"

"Yeah, so-what?" I answered.

"Well, compared to what you're stuck with, my girl's fuckin' great. Sorry about yours."

"What to you mean, 'your' girl?" I retorted. “She was lookin' at me."

"Lookin' at you? She was lookin' at me the whole time." David upended the bottle and took a gulp. "Whew! Powerful medicine," he hissed and handed me the bottle. "Here, this'll make your girl look fuckin' beautiful."

I looked at the bottle of clear bootleg whiskey in my hand. Since I was rapidly getting into a 'what-the-hell' kind of mood, I took a healthy swig and held it in my mouth for a moment. Then, I let the searing liquid slip down my throat, scorch my vocal cords, and roar into my intestines. "Oh, shit," I rasped.

"Great stuff, isn't it?" David announced hoarsely. "Take another one."

I fought down another swallow. My body rebelled and I would've gagged it up had it not been for my ego not wishing me to barf in front of Petey. David grabbed the bottle away from me and took another big swallow. Petey took a turn without a reaction. I imagined his throat was nothing but thick scar tissue, since he was probably weaned on the nasty shit since birth.

David thumped his chest like Tarzan again and gave a short jungle call. The whiskey hit my bloodstream and my head started to spin. "Man," I wheezed, "I can feel it already." David quickly shoved the bottle at my mouth like he was feeding a baby calf. I took a swallow and forced it down.

David held the bottle up toward the glow coming around the barn from the parking lot and pronounced, "Well, that's it folks. Just one more bolt of lightning left for the evil sinners." He leaned in close to me and switched into his conspiratorial mode, raised the bottle and whispered in my ear, "Here's to watermelon tits. May they be suckable and their owner be fuckable." Then with great flair he gulped down the last slug of whiskey and threw the empty bottle in a long arc off into the dark woods. "Dead soldier," he said with mock sadness and turned to Petey. "Hey, Petey, what'll we do now?"

Petey shrugged. The rotgut whiskey was having its effect on all three of us, especially me. "Let's go back inside," I said.

"No, not yet," David ordered. I could see his cockeyed mind spinning into action. "Hey, I know what," he brightened. "The game!"

"Oh, shit," I said. "What now? What game?"

David turned to Petey. "Remember the game you showed me last summer?" Petey grinned wide at David. I was surprised he could remember anything beyond five minutes, let alone last summer. And then, I wondered what else Petey had shown him last summer.

"What game?" I demanded.

"You'll see. Come on, follow me," David said and headed off in the shadows toward the rear of the barn. "It's called, 'see-the-bird'," he shouted over his shoulder as Petey and I hurried after him.

The moon was almost overhead and illuminated a large clearing behind the barn. The land fell away down a slope to a small marsh that bled off into the woods beyond. Just at the edge of a large clump of cattails was an outhouse raised up on lattice covered stilts that brought it even with the top of the slope, where a short, narrow ramp led to the wooden door that actually had a half-moon cut in it like the cartoons. Down Maine art, I thought to myself.

Feeling the gathering effects of Maine's best moonshine rapidly poisoning my system, I followed David and Petey down to the base of the outhouse. "What's going on?" I asked.

"Shhhh, keep your voice down," David ordered sharply. "First, we get us a long cattail," he whispered and ripped one out of the clump of cattails next to the lattice covered stilts.

I watched as Petey pulled back several pieces of the lattice and broke them off, leaving an open space.

"What're you guys gonna do?" I whispered to David.

"We're gonna wait for...a bird," he giggled.

"A bird?"

"You haven't seen anything like this in your whole life," he said and gave Petey a devilish look.

"He'ah comes one," Petey whispered, looking off toward a door that had just opened at the rear of the barn. Outlined in the doorway was a young woman.

"Okay," David said in a hushed voice, trying to stifle his laughter, "we gotta keep quiet or we'll scare it away."

The woman closed the door and walked the short distance to the ramp. Down below, the three of us hunkered in close to the lattice as she crossed the ramp to the outhouse and went inside. Then, it suddenly dawned on me what was going on and I started to snicker. David looked at me and nodded his head excitedly. I slapped my hand over my mouth to stop myself from laughing out loud.

David quietly rose up next to the lattice and peered up through the opening Petey had made in the slats.

"You're not gonna..." I whispered.

"Shhh," David hushed. "Come'ere." He pulled me

in next to him and pointed at the hole. "Look," he mouthed.

I looked up through the hole in the slats. A rim of light from inside the outhouse framed the woman's bare rear end as she sat on the wooden toilet seat.

David breathed excitedly into my ear, "See the bird?"

I looked up into the pitch black cavern beneath the one-holer and, lo and behold, there it was. Unmistakable. Right there in silhouette between the woman's legs, exactly what David had described. The bird, in all its furry glory.

David eased me back away from the hole in the lattice and moved in. Very gently, like an Indian getting ready to spear a salmon, he eased the long cattail up through the opening. I looked at Petey. For someone with eyes as dull as a dead rat's, he stood there next to us full of half-witted anticipation.

I inched in closer to David. He waited for just the right moment to strike. Then, I heard it, the unmistakable sound of pee splattering down on the dung-heap hole inside the lattice. David thrust up hard and true. The woman let out a terrified scream from above that split the night air like a banshee. David jerked the cattail back and the three of us hunkered down in the darkness. The door to the outhouse flew open with a bang. The petrified woman tripped out onto the ramp with her underpants down around her ankles. She uttered shrill panicked gasps as she pulled her urine-splattered panties up under her dress and ran back into the barn.

When the barn door slammed shut, the three of us literally came apart. David fell right to the ground, convulsing and snorting like a pig, which was how he sounded when he laughed uncontrollably. "I got one!" ...snort... "I got one!" ...snort-snort... "Did you see'er?... She...she pissed all over herself." ...snort-snort-snort-snort.

Aided by the 150 proof hooch, I laughed so hard I couldn't catch my breath and started rolling over and over, holding my aching stomach, and gasping for air. Petey sat on his rump and grabbed tightly onto the toes of his worn-out sneakers. His skinny, parchment-skinned face crinkled up and his pig eyes disappeared into the creases. He laughed in short high-pitched cackles like an hysterical hyena. That made David and me laugh even harder. So much so, that it took us another fifteen minutes to pull ourselves together. Finally we wiped the tears from our eyes and headed back up the slope to the barn dance.

We walked right through the whitewashed horse stall and into the barn without showing old 'Mrs. Red Gums' the black X's she'd stamped on our hands. I had a hunch she knew who we were.

Inside the barn, several couples were slumped together, dancing to a dated slow number under the dim lights. Most of the others were slouched on some benches stashed against the walls or seated at several old folding card tables scattered around the dancing area. None of them looked as if they were talking to each other or having anything close to a good time. Probably ran out of things to say to each other years ago.

Over under the hayloft, the woman who David had skewered with the cattail was talking anxiously in hushed tones with two other young women. I tried to imagine what the hell she thought was lurking down under the toilet seat, but gave up. I was beginning to realize that anything resembling a normal imagination had, most likely, been inbred out centuries ago. I looked down to my right, just inside the door. I shouldn't have. A dumpy hag in a faded cloth, colorless dress was slumped on a bench staring up at me through dull, suspicious eyes, as she dug deep into a nostril. Without taking her eyes off me, she pulled out the prize she was after and popped it into her mouth like an Orpheum Theater Raisinet. It was a good thing David spotted the girls at that moment or I would've heaved right there on the spot.

"Time to make my move," David declared to me out of the side of his mouth.

I looked across the slumping dancers to where Sandy was leaning against a tall, gaunt, mean looking guy with frightening black eyes that glowered from deep within two hollows set in his skull. There was something familiar about him. Shit. The guy from the parking lot social club who'd stared at me. He had his long arm slung around Sandy's shoulder with his hand precariously close to one of her prominent features. Without the guy seeing her, she looked our way and gave us a 'warning' look. Mildred stood next to Sandy. Alone.

"She's lookin' at me," David breathed into my ear. "J'you see that? I'm goin' over."

"Who's that with'er?" I cautioned, instinctively knowing that David didn't sense the danger I felt. He never did.

"My cousin, Ira," Petey muttered. I looked at him. He had a deep frown knitted into his pale forehead.

"Is he her boyfriend?" David asked Petey.

Petey hesitated a moment. That gave it away. "Kinda," he mumbled.

David's eyes flashed, which was always a bad sign.

"Hey, he's no match for DAH-veed-zee-magnificent!" he bragged. "Watch this, Billy-boy."

David pumped himself up mentally and ambled across the dance floor toward Sandy. I glanced at Petey again. There was an anxiety in his tiny little eyes, as he watched David, which made me uncomfortable. I left Petey by the door and followed after David.

David stopped a few feet from Sandy. I saw her shoot him a look of caution. I was glad he took it. The guy she was leaning against was much fiercer looking at close range. David quickly downshifted into his nonchalant act and walked up to Mildred. "Wanna dance?" he asked, as if they were old friends.

Skinny little Mildred's arms tightened involuntarily across her caved-in chest. She looked at David in shock. Probably stunned that anyone would even notice she existed, let alone want to dance with her. David started to ask her again, but she interrupted with a weak stutter, "Y-Yeah..."

David gave Sandy one of his 'all-knowing-I-got-your-message' looks and headed for the dance floor with Mildred following meekly behind him.

I stood there; a few feet away from Sandy and her kinda-boyfriend, watching David and Mildred fumble around. The poor thing didn't even know where to put her hands. Then, as I watched the two of them awkwardly step-together-step, I felt an overwhelming urge to look back at Sandy. I did. She was staring right into my eyes. Again I cursed myself, as the blood rushed into my face. I abruptly looked away, just as the two other creepy parking lot drinking partners walked across my sight path up to Petey's cousin, Ira. One of them grinned a toothless grin at

Ira and pulled a full bottle of vintage rotgut out of his shirt. Ira unslung his long arm from around Sandy. "I'm goin' outside," he told her in a low, rasping 'don't mess with me' voice. "You wait he'ah."

"Drinkin'?" Sandy asked flatly.

Ira glared at her with one of the most evil and menacing looks I'd ever seen. "Ye'ah, whudda'bout it?" he growled.

She glared hard right back at him. "Nothin'."

The dancers on the floor made way for Ira and his buddies, as they walked straight through them and out of the barn.

I felt a slight dryness creep into my throat and wished I had a slug of Petey's hooch available. I looked across the dance floor. David and Mildred were still step-together-stepping over in front of the bandstand. David looked miserable. Mildred had rigor mortis. I spotted Petey, who was under the loft watching me watch him. I decided to wait it out where I was.

"Would you like to dance?"

The words sent a spine-tingling chill through me. I'd just watched the meanest man in the world leave the building and now his 'kinda' girlfriend was asking me if I wanted to dance with her. I turned around and there she was standing right in front of me. Looking right up into my eyes, with a bright, radiant smile on her face. "Um..." I think I said. Then, before I could elaborate, she slipped her small hand into mine and we were headed onto the dance floor. My heart was pounding so hard inside my chest it hurt.

We reached the center of the barn, where most of the strung-together lights were concentrated overhead.

Great. Right where everyone in this weird, alien world could see us. Sandy automatically turned her body into mine. I could feel her firm breasts through my thin summer shirt. I'd never really felt anything like it before. Not that I hadn't danced close with anyone. I had. But, somehow, it was different.

Sandy didn't seem like the girls back home. Nothing seemed like back home. She snuggled her head into the crook of my shoulder and wrapped her free arm firmly around my neck. Sandy was in command. I definitely was not. We really didn't dance, just sort of swayed to the slow rhythm the band was playing. I felt like a five-foot-ten-inch immovable fire hydrant.

"Which one are you?" she cooed into my ear.

"Billy."

"You're cute."

I could feel her warm breath on my cheek. "Thanks...ah...so're you..."

She nuzzled my cheek and nestled into my shoulder again, as she fitted her body into mine. My face must have been beet red. And, I didn't have my school books to cover myself. Perspiration began beading up on my forehead. I stared up at the overhead lightbulbs, trying to think of something that would stop the incredible throbbing between my legs. Anything. Baseball. Big Red. Nothing worked. I happened to glance over under the loft. Petey was quietly staring at us. The frown I'd seen before was still there. We began to turn, as we swayed to the music.

Several yards away, David was step-together-stepping at arms length with Mildred and glaring wide-eyed at Sandy and me in complete disbelief. Suddenly, something inside me rushed to the surface and, before I knew I'd done it, I grinned back at David in 'triumph.' Then, to rub it in, I took control and glided Sandy around in a circle under the lights and on over near to where David was stopped in his tracks, a flabbergasted look on his face. I gave him one of his own big, exaggerated winks. His expression began to change.

A cloud came over him, an ominous darkness that I couldn't define. There was something new in his eyes. Something I'd never seen before. Something different... I eased Sandy around in a circle and guided her back toward the middle of the barn. Abruptly, the music stopped. The square dance caller blurted something into the tinny microphone, making me jump. Sandy giggled and looked up at me.

"Okay. S'time fo'ah'nuth'ah do-si-do. Grab yo'ah pahtnah."

The embalmed dancers began to form up into squares. I hesitated. I guess Sandy felt the panic inside me and led me over to where Petey was leaning against a support timber under the loft. I saw Petey shoot Sandy a quick look of disapproval. She just flashed her eyes belligerently right back at him.

Just then, David sauntered up with Mildred tagging sullenly along behind him. He ignored me and spoke pointedly right at Sandy, "Wanna dance?"

"You can't square dance," I said to David, feeling the friction mounting between us.

David didn't even bother to look at me. He just pinned Sandy, waiting for her answer. Sandy looked right into his eyes and smiled very sweetly. "I'm taken." Then, she slipped her hand into mine and pulled me away toward the dance floor.

"Wait a minute," I whispered to her, "I don't know how to..."

"I'll teach you," she said and squeezed my hand tightly in hers. We formed up with three other humanoid couples, who just stared at me like I was from another planet. I was.

The band jump-started a fast number. The caller sputtered his rapid-fire square dance calls into the ancient Electro-Voice microphone that made him sound like an old 78 rpm record. I immediately went the wrong way and smashed right into the oncoming dancers. They didn't think it was funny. Sandy jerked me back around, but it was too late. I'd crunched someone's instep. That was it. I had failed the rural down Maine square dancing test. Sandy pulled me out of the oncoming traffic. "I told you I didn't know how," I said, beet red again.

"Hey, it's okay. S'no matter."

I looked over under the loft. Petey was still there, but David and Mildred had disappeared. That's all I needed. Being stranded at the 'Dead Man's Ball' wasn't my idea of a good time. Sandy and I walked over to Petey.

"Where's David?" I asked.

"Outside with Mildred," he mumbled flatly and shot Sandy another look.

"Let's go find'em," she said defiantly.

Petey squinted her a warning with his beady eyes. "You with him?" he asked her with a nod of his shrunken head toward me.

"Yeah," she fired back, "what of it?"

"Best not."

"Best too," she hissed at Petey and then ordered

me to, "Come on."

"Wait-what's wrong?" I asked Petey, with far too much trepidation in my voice.

Petey didn't look at me - just stared at Sandy. "She knows," he muttered.

"I don't know nothin', Petey Peak," she shot back and then glared at me with fire in her dark eyes. "You comin'?"

I watched as Sandy turned abruptly and marched out of the barn. I hesitated next to Petey who just stared vacantly through the dancing ghosts at the open door to the whitewashed front room. "She knows," he uttered somberly under his breath. I could see the sense of dread in his jaundiced eyes and decided I'd be better off following Sandy out of the barn. I didn't have much choice.

I stepped out onto the small landing just outside the door to the whitewashed stall. Sandy was sitting on the bottom step with her arms around her knees. She seemed smaller than she had inside. I waited for her to look around at me. She didn't. "You alright?" I finally asked.

"Yeah," she answered very softly, without moving.

I stepped down off the landing and walked a few feet out in front of her. Without turning, I pretended to look for David and Mildred. "You see where they went?"

"In your car."

I turned around. She was resting her chin in her hands and looking off into the darkness of the woods beside the barn. Her eyes seemed distant and sad.

"Um...it's not mine... It's David's. I...I don't have my license yet."

She looked up at me. Her eyes seemed to search

mine for a long moment. I shrugged, a little embarrassed at being fifteen and not having a goddamned thing to say. Then, she abruptly stood up, reached out, and grabbed me by my hand.

"Come on," she said. The spark came back into her voice, and she led me off in the direction of the station wagon.

As we hurried through the parked cars, Sandy didn't notice the shadowy figure of Cyrus Peak watching us from the woods. I did. The sight of his dark, hunched figure, standing there among the trees, gave me the willies.

David was sitting behind the steering wheel with Mildred squeezed up tight against her door, as far away from him as she could get. As we walked up to the driver's side of the station wagon, I could see that David was still in a foul mood; so I decided to attempt to smooth over his ruffled feathers as if nothing had happened. "Hey, what's goin' on here?" I teased.

David gave me a surly sidelong glance and muttered under his breath, "We're just fuckin' procreating all over the fuckin' place." I ignored the slam and opened the backdoor to let Sandy in.

"How's the fuckin' square dance champion?" David shot.

Obviously, my attempt at making peace hadn't worked. Whenever David used the word 'fuck' three consecutive times, it meant that he was really pissed off. I slipped in next to Sandy and closed the door. Silence filled the car for several long minutes.

Finally, David mumbled, "Open some beers."

As I reached back over the rear seat and took four beers out of the cooler, a strange thought flitted through my mind. Maybe, it was because David was being such a shithead and overusing his favorite expletive that I remembered the first time we discovered the word fuck...

...I never really went for the word like David did. He was already eight, and me nearly seven, when we found it scrawled on the old bridge over the river where we used to swim. Just four benign letters of our alphabet that, when tossed together, make up one of the most powerful words in the universal language of man. And, depending on the inflection and reason, it's a four-letter word that has the potential to trigger anything from a minor tiff to an all-out world war. Little did we know that day how enlightened we would become. However, when we got back to David's house, and he asked his mother what 'F-U-C-K' spelled, we got our first clue. I think that was the first time I was present at one of David's ear-boxing sessions. She ordered David to never 'ever' use that word again. But, quite to the contrary, his mother's harsh reaction had exactly the opposite effect on her son. It only succeeded in awakening him to the fact that he'd just added one of the strongest weapons yet to his mental arsenal. Even though we hadn't the damnedest idea of what the hell it meant.

David's mandatory follow-up session with the good Reverend Stevens didn't produce much information as to what was so abhorrent about the word. So, David consulted a couple of the older and wiser kids on the school playground, who willingly enlightened and illuminated us. When David realized its true meaning, he became totally unglued. It was as if he alone had discovered the secret of creation. And I suppose, upon reflection, he just may have. I, on the other hand, hadn't quite grasped the full context of the playground student lecture, but decided not to tell my mother about our discovery. Although she'd never boxed my ears, I felt that discretion was the better part of valor in that particular instance...

"Me an' Billy are goin' out for varsity football this year. I'm gonna be the quarterback and Billy's gonna be my end."

"What?" I asked, snapping out of it.

"I was just tellin' Mildred here about us goin' out for football." His attempt at returning to his charming self.

"Oh..." I uttered and looked at Sandy sitting beside me. She was holding her opened beer in her lap and staring absently out the window. I listened, as David slugged down a gulp of beer and gave Mildred a rapid-fire description of 'our' future football plans.

"I didn't go out for it before, 'cause I wasn't heavy enough."

...Lie. He hadn't gone out for football because his mother was afraid he'd get hurt...

"But, I've been workin' out with weights an' eatin' a lot of protein."

...Another lie... The fact was, I had been working out in the school weight room for over six months. David had shown up only once, did a few twenty pound curls and bullshitted me about nailing one of his private school girls. He never showed his face in the weight room again. In fact, he'd seemed annoyed that I'd started spending so much time there; something that really puzzled me, because he kept telling everyone at Vic's pepper steak shop about how he was going out for varsity quarterback. He had the little All Saints girls eating it up...

"Oh," Mildred uttered timidly.

"I put on eight pounds in three months."

...From all the beer and French fries I thought to myself, not from working out and eating protein...

David rolled up the short sleeve of his checkered shirt and doubled his bicep into a knotted ball. "Feel that," he demanded. Mildred tentatively touched his flexed bicep with her bony finger and quickly pulled back into her protective arm-wrap.

"Pretty good, huh?" he asked Mildred, as he twisted his fist back and forth, making his bicep pop up and down.

"Yes," Mildred uttered shyly.

"Fuckin-A, man. Like a fuckin' ball of steel." David rolled his sleeve back down and looked out his window for a long moment, then slugged down the rest of his beer. I couldn't see his face in the rearview mirror, but I heard him crush the aluminum can in his hands. I ducked as he tossed it back, just missing my head.

"Hey! What's the matter with you?" I snapped.

"Nothin'...friend," he answered flatly without turning around.

I decided not to play into his drama and turned to Sandy. She was still staring out at the darkness. "Anything wrong?" I asked. She just shook her head slightly and continued to look out the window. Silence filled the car.

Petey's backwoods hooch had given my brain a ticket to ride a roller coaster and the beer on top of that wasn't exactly doing my equilibrium any good. I rested my head on the seat and closed my eyes, trying to steady my thoughts for a few minutes...

...*Patricia*... *Patricia* hadn't run out of the Orpheum after all. The gum-snapper wasn't there either. *Patricia* sat in the seat beside me and rested her head on my shoulder. Her hair was soft and silky and smelled like fresh air. Slowly, I turned. We looked at each other for a long moment. There was a knowing worldliness in her dark brown eyes that belied her years. Almost a sadness that said she already knew too much for someone so young. Slowly, her lips brushed mine and a shiver ran through my body. She pulled back and looked at me again, searching for something. Then, she reached up and gently touched my cheek with her fingertips. Her lips pressed against mine. Blood rushed from my heart, through my body, and swirled up into my head. Her lips were soft and moist as they moved slowly over mine... Since I was about twelve, I had kissed several different girls, but never like... never like...*Patricia*... Sandy...pulled away and rested her head on my shoulder again... *I looked back at the movie screen...* A strip of light sliced across someone's angry eyes, as they stared back at me from the reflection in the...rearview mirror. David's eyes. David was staring right at me in the rearview mirror. He had watched Sandy kiss me. He glared at me with disdain for a moment, then snorted and reached over and jerked Mildred into him.

"You really can kiss," Sandy whispered to me.

David snorted again and started roughly French kissing Mildred, who sat there like a terrified mouse and took it.

Sandy looked at me again. My senses were trying hard to break through the swirl in my head. She eased the can of beer from my hand and set it on the floorboard. Then, ever-so-slowly, she took my hand and placed it firmly over one of her breasts, all the while looking right into my eyes. My heart pounded out of control. The racing roller coaster plunged down into a gut-wrenching slide, then careened wildly upwards and whipped around a sharp turn at breakneck speed. "Yes, Billy. Yes," she whispered.

I could feel the cold perspiration springing out of the pores on my face. We kissed again. Her mouth opened slowly and her warm tongue explored passionately inside mine, as she held my hand to her warm breast. The pressure in my head felt like my skull was going to explode. I eased my hand from under hers and started to slip it up beneath her white peasant blouse. Just as my fingers felt the curve of her bra, she clutched my wrist and moved my hand away. "No, Billy," she breathed into my ear, "not here."

I tilted my head back and looked at her. Then, I saw why she had stopped me. She was glaring at David's reflected eyes in the rearview mirror. He'd been watching us the whole time. David quickly looked away and started impassively kissing Mildred again.

...You're a real scumbag, David, I thought to myself. Geez, I couldn't remember ever being all that bothered by very much of anything David had done before. I had usually just brushed it off or chalked it up to his intricately scattered mind. But, the fact was, there had been a strange new feeling of alienation growing inside me about him that I couldn't explain and couldn't make go away. I'm not sure, but I think it began just after Patricia saw me in the Orpheum passion pit, and ran out of the theater...

The bright headlights swept through the station wagon from behind us and whipped around as an old black pickup truck roared into the parking lot and slid to a stop in front of the barn.

Horrified, Sandy broke away from me and looked out her window. "Oh, Jesus," she whispered loudly, "it's Ira." She glared wide-eyed at David, who looked back at her baffled. "We gotta get the hell outta here," she rasped in a panic.

I looked over her through the car window and saw Ira and his two drunken buddies stumble out of the pickup and head for the barn. Mildred hunkered down on the front seat, terrified. Sandy reached over me and grabbed David by his shirt.

"Hurry!" she shouted. "If he sees me, we'll really be in for it."

"Alright-alright," David stammered and started the car. He jammed the gears into reverse, spun gravel and wheeled the station wagon out of the parking lot. As we hit the paved road with a screech, I looked back at the barn and caught sight of Petey silhouetted in the open doorway - watching us leave.

The moon had dipped below the tree line. It was pitch black. None of us spoke, as we sped over the dark backwoods road. The station wagon's headlights pierced through the darkness. Sandy and I kept looking back to see if anyone was following us. Her kinda-boyfriend must be one mean bastard; I thought to myself and instantly wished I hadn't. The car hit a big rut in the road and bounced us up to the roof. David slowed down.

"Faster!" Sandy yelled at him.

"Where're we supposed to be going?" David shouted back at her.

"My house."

"Where the hell is it?"

"Just keep goin'," she snapped. "I'll tell you when to turn."

"Fuckin' roads all look alike," David grumbled, as he maneuvered the station wagon through a chain of sharp curves.

"Turn here," Sandy suddenly shouted.

Without slowing down, David whipped the steering wheel sharply to the left and careened wildly onto a lone, rutted dirt drive. "Oh, shit!" he blurted out, as he lost control of the car. The station wagon slid sideways along the soft shoulder, spraying dirt and rocks off into the darkness.

"Watch out for the bridge!" Sandy screamed out.

David desperately grabbed at the spinning steering wheel. The car whipped around backwards and slid crazily onto a narrow, rickety wooden bridge, then smashed tail-first through the guardrail. My head slammed up hard against the steel roof, filling my brain with a million white stars.

The next thing I knew, I was jammed down onto the floor, crunched up against the back of the front seat. Sandy was squeezed down on top of me, almost crushing the air out of my lungs. The car seemed to be tilted up at a sharp angle and there was water leaking in through the rear hatch.

Sandy struggled away from me in the darkness. "You stupid bastard," she yelled at David, who was untangling himself from the steering wheel.

"Why didn't you give me a fucking warning, for crissakes?" he shot back at her.

I pulled myself back up onto the slanted back seat

and caught my breath. "Anyone hurt?" I asked.

Mildred pulled herself out from underneath the dashboard and whimpered pathetically, "My eye... I hurt my eye..."

"Oh, great," Sandy blurted out. "You stupid jerk," she fired at David and shoved her door open. Water rushed inside from the shallow creek we'd landed in. "Come on, Mildred," Sandy commanded and stepped out into the running spring water.

David and I pushed our doors open and got out knee-deep into the creek. Sandy opened Mildred's door and took her by her free hand. Mildred's other hand covered her wounded eye. We hauled ourselves up onto the narrow bridge. "God!" David exclaimed, as he looked at his station wagon, with its front wheels grasping onto the bridge and its tail end submerged in about two feet of water. With its headlights staring up into the night sky, it looked like a wounded dinosaur. "We'll never get it out," David uttered in disbelief.

I looked over at Sandy. She was standing with Mildred in the bright beam of a headlight, trying to examine Mildred's eye. "Take your hand away," she demanded. Mildred obediently complied. Sandy took a closer look.

"She okay?" David asked, shaken.

"No. Thanks to you," Sandy shot back.

"Hey, man, you were the one who had to go so fucking fast."

"Come off it," I interrupted. "What'll we do now?"

We all spotted the oncoming headlights at the same time, sweeping through the curves, about a quarter of a mile back down the road.

"Me an' Mildred are goin' on up to my house, you best come too," Sandy said quickly.

"What about my car?" David asked nervously. "Shit, I just can't fuckin' leave it here."

Sandy started to lead Mildred away, just as a pickup truck swerved off the road onto the drive and headed right toward us. In one motion, Ira Peak jammed on the brakes and stepped out of the pickup, like he was dismounting a horse. His deep black, menacing eyes drilled Sandy. "What'da hell you doin', girl?" he seethed.

The other door of the pickup truck opened and Petey got out. He shuffled around to the front and leaned on the battered fender.

"What the hell's it look like?" Sandy answered, standing her ground.

Ira weaved his tall, lanky frame drunkenly in front of her. "Don't give me no fuckin' lip or I'll knock yo'ah goddamned head off. What'chu doin' with these boys?"

I could see the glint of violence rising from deep within Ira's black eye-pits. My knees started to shake inside my soaked jeans. Sandy quickly went on the defensive. "They're just givin' us a ride home. You left, remember? Now, get lost."

Petey stepped over to David. "What happened?" he mumbled.

Seeing the trace of fear in David's eyes, Sandy jumped in. "It was my fault. I didn't tell'im about the bridge in time."

"Dumb bitch," Ira uttered under his breath.

Petey walked over next to Ira. "Let's pull'em out," he muttered.

Ira glared at David and me standing in the bright

headlights of the pickup. Then without saying anything, he and Petey hooked up the cable from the winch on the front end of the pickup to the front axle under the station wagon.

"Steer it," Petey said to David.

David scrambled down into the water and quickly got in behind the steering wheel of his drowning car. Ira fired up his pickup and the winch whined and pulled the wounded station wagon slowly back up onto the groaning old bridge.

Petey unhooked the cable and fed it back onto the winch. David jumped out of the righted station wagon. With a mixture of panic and relief on his face, he stepped nervously over to Ira in the pickup. "Hey, thanks for..." he started to say. Ira snapped him a warning look, hit the accelerator and gunned the pickup back off the bridge. Spun the truck around and roared off into the night, spraying gravel on everyone as he left.

I just stood there, feeling my shocked body fluids beginning to flow again.

"Will you drive me an' Mildred up to the house?" Sandy asked David. She was noticeably subdued.

"Yeah-sure," David answered and got into the car.

I opened the rear door for Sandy and Mildred "Ah...thanks for covering for us," I managed to say to Sandy, as she helped Mildred into the back seat. She gave me kind of a sad little smile, then glanced at Petey. A look passed between them. What it meant, I couldn't really tell. It was different than the ones before. More of a feeling. An understanding. Sandy got in the back with Mildred. I sat with Petey in the front with David.

The long dirt drive led to a small, dimly lit,

ramshackle house set in the middle of a field of stubble and stumps. The front yard was overgrown with dead chaff and strewn with rusting car parts, an old roller-type washer, and other scattered junk. David pulled up near the front door. A tattered curtain covered the cracked-glass front window. Any paint that had once preserved the wooden exterior had long since evaporated into the past. A light was on inside.

Sandy got out, holding Mildred's hand. "You boys comin' in?" she asked us rather nicely.

Without saying a word, David, Petey, and I got out of the car and followed Sandy and Mildred into the dilapidated house. The kitchen-living room was lighted by a single bulb that hung by a frayed cord from the yellowish ceiling. Cracked linoleum covered most of the old board floor. There was an outmoded cast iron oil cooking stove off to one side with a black crook-necked smokestack stabbed through the plasterboard wall, which was layered with years of grease and grime. Pretty barren except for a bunch of colorful wildflowers arranged in a Ball Mason Jar on the Formica kitchen table.

My eyes went right to a middle-aged, jut-jawed woman. She was slouched in a filthy, moth-eaten, overstuffed chair set right in front of a battered metal black-and-white television set with a bent rabbit ears antenna sticking out of it. The grayish light from the picture, of whatever she was watching, flickered onto her gaunt, sallow face. Slowly, she lifted her bone-thin, blue-veined hand, which was hanging straight down over the thick arm of the chair, holding a half-smoked cigarette pinched between nicotine stained fingers. She brought the cigarette up to her thin, cracked lips and, without taking her eyes off the television set, sucked so hard that her cheeks caved in and almost touched each other. When she exhaled, hardly any smoke came out.

Sandy left us standing just inside the door and led Mildred to a small kitchen sink built into a chipped pressboard cupboard set against the far wall. As she cleared some dirty pans and dishes out of the stained sink, she introduced us. "Ma, that's Billy an' David. You know Petey. Mildred hurt her eye."

The woman didn't take her pale, vacant eyes off the television set or acknowledge us in any way that I could see. Sandy wet a soiled dishcloth and made a compress for Mildred's eye, which was rapidly turning black-and-blue and swelling shut. Then, she left Mildred holding the compress to her eye and headed for a door to another room. "Back in a minute," she said and disappeared.

We just stood there watching Mildred dab at her swollen eye.

"You boys visitin'?" The woman's throat-rattling twang startled me. Too many cigarettes and years of sloshing down rotgut. Both David and I stared at her for a moment without answering. She still hadn't looked at us.

"Ah...yes...we're up here for a couple of days," David said with somewhat of a rattle in his own throat.

The woman's eyes shifted to our wet jeans and shoes. "Whud'appened?" she gurgled.

David looked down at his wet shoes, then at me. I just shrugged. "Well," David said, "I didn't see your bridge back there and..."

"Been drinkin'?" she interrupted.

David gave me a quizzical look, then answered, "Just ah...just a couple of beers."

The woman's expressionless eyes drifted back to the droning television set and she took another long suck on her cigarette.

Sandy walked back into the room and checked Mildred's eye. "Where's Pa?" Sandy asked her mother as she picked up the jar of wildflowers and added some water from the dripping faucet over the sink.

"Down'ta' the boat drinkin'," was the unemotional throat-rattling response.

Sandy set the flowers back on the table and went to the grime-covered cupboard and took down a carton of baking soda. She shook some onto the wet towel compress and carefully placed it back onto Mildred's black eye. "You stayin' the night, Mildred?" she asked. Mildred nodded. Sandy turned to us. "Thanks for the ride home," she said brightly, as if nothing had happened.

"Yeah-sure," David said. "Ah...well... see you around."

As David and Petey went back outside, I glanced at Sandy. She smiled but said nothing, so I started after them.

"Billy," Sandy said softly.

I stopped halfway through the door. "Yeah?"

Sandy walked up close to me and looked into my eyes. "Will I see you tomorrow?" she whispered.

I felt the old out-of-control blood rush to my face, but didn't have time to curse myself. "Sure...what...what time?" I managed to ask. Then, I saw her mother watching us from her chair. Her eyes were as cold as ice.

"I'll be at the store around ten," Sandy said sweetly.

"Okay, I'll see you there," I answered with more than a little catch in my throat.

"You're nice, Billy."

She studied my face for a moment, then reached up and lightly touched my cheek. I was pretty sure I was beet red. "Bye," she said to me in a low, hushed voice.

We looked at each other for a long moment, until David broke the silence. "You comin'?" he called sharply from over next to the station wagon.

"Yeah," I answered, without taking my eyes off Sandy. Then, I turned to leave, but caught a glimpse of Sandy's mother in the chair. She gave Sandy a hard look then turned back to the television set.

Sandy closed the door behind me and I hurried over to the station wagon. David was already behind the wheel. As I went around to the other side and opened the door to get in the front, I passed Petey who was getting in the back. "Best not," he uttered to me under his breath and slammed the door shut.

Without saying a word, David wheeled the car around and drove back along the drive and over the wooden bridge with its splintered guardrail dangling down into the creek. As we turned onto the main road, I barely noticed the dark form of a pickup truck parked down off the shoulder. There was the outline of a winch on the front end. I felt a cold shudder run through me, but didn't say anything.

On the way back to the cottage, David dropped Petey off by a rusting RFD mailbox hung on a split rail pole next to a dirt drive that disappeared off into the woods. No one had said a word since we'd left Sandy's, so I guessed it must have led to wherever Petey lived.

It was very dark back at the cottage. We'd forgotten to leave any lights on. David got out of the station wagon without speaking and went right into the house. I sat in the car for a moment. I was too tired to have a confrontation and knew David was sending every signal he could that that was exactly what he wanted. At least, my head had gotten off the roller coaster ride. The backflip off the bridge and Sandy's kinda-boyfriend, Ira Peak, had seen to that.

The light went on in the living room. Big Red raced out of the opened door and unloaded onto one of his selection of trees. Then, he ran up to my side of the station wagon and whined excitedly for me to get out of the car. With Big Red running and jumping happily around me and in my path, I begrudgingly went inside.

David was already in the bedroom, stripped to his shorts and getting into his sleeping bag on the other twin bed. He still wasn't speaking. Only Big Red was thrilled that I was there. So, since David was being a major jerk, I took it upon myself to feed Big Red a big bowl of the dog food we'd bought at the general store and gave him some clean water. Then, I got a cold soda from the refrigerator and sat at the kitchen table waiting for Big Red to finish chowing down, knowing he'd want out for a minute to revisit his trees before we both called it a night.

With Big Red curled up on the braided rug between the twin beds, and both David and me in our respective sleeping bags, everything seemed almost normal again. David had his sleeping bag pulled up over his head pretending to be asleep. I reached over and turned out the lamp on the bedside table and laid my head on my pillow and closed my eyes. The smell of fresh pine wafted in through the slightly opened window and reminded me of the YMCA summer camp, on Lake Winnipesauke in New Hampshire, that David and I went to when I was nine...

...One morning, after breakfast in the large open air chow hall, David had gotten caught lighting off a stink bomb under the junior counselors' cabin and had to spend the rest of the day sitting outside the camp director's office. I snuck him candy bars and a comic book, when no one was looking. David swore that he'd get even with the director someday; and, I suppose he did in a way. We didn't go back the next year, because David told his mother there was nest of poisonous snakes under our cabin...

"Well, score one for your side," David uttered in the darkness of the bedroom, breaking my spell.

"What?" I mumbled, instinctively knowing that David had worked out his confrontation strategy and was putting it into play.

"I could've had her. I just got diverted."

"Yeah," I said, without any inflection. One of David's big deals was always having to save face. And, since I was the one who had made the points with Sandy, it was his way of justifying the fact that things hadn't gone his way.

"Yeah," he answered, with more of an edge than I'd expected because David would usually just make his bravado excuse, then drop the subject. "That's right," he went on, "she was lookin' at me the whole time."

I rolled over in my sleeping bag and pulled it up over my head.

"I saw the boob job you were givin'er. Hey, I'm proud of you son. I didn't know you had it in you," David teased, trying to bait me. Then, he started laughing lasciviously.

"Blow off," I said.

"Oooooo," David goaded, "touchy-touchy. Maybe tomorrow you'll make your big move."

I sat up. "Shut up, David."

He didn't answer. I lay back down. The only sound was Big Red's heavy breathing from the middle of the braided rug. I started to close my eyes and, actually, thought David might have been getting back to his normal sick-humored self, with even the possibility of conceding me a point or two. I couldn't have been more wrong.

"You think you'll even know what to do?" David said caustically in the dark. I shed my sleeping bag and leaped off my bed. Big Red jumped straight up out of a sound sleep. I grabbed David's mattress and flipped it and him onto the floor. David scrambled out of his sleeping bag.

"Oh-oh," he said, as he threw back the mattress. "So, the big stud wants a fight?" Then, David came at me with a flying tackle that sent us both down onto the other twin bed.

Big Red barked furiously as we both grappled in the dark, each trying to get a good hold on the other. We rolled off the bed in a double bear hug and landed with a thud onto the floor, just missing Big Red who sprang out of the way and barked even more at us.

We grunted and groaned in the clinch until my six months of weight training overcame David's grip, and I was able to break free and shove him back hard against a large chest of drawers. We were both out of breath and, for an instant, I thought the fight was over. How dumb. David had braced himself against the chest and, as I sat up to catch my wind, his legs snapped around my head in a vice-like scissor-lock that took me back down to the floor. I gripped his ankles and tried to pry them loose, but David had me and knew it.

"Think you're a big man 'cause you got Sandy," he gritted through clinched teeth, trying to tighten the 'jaws-of-death' around my skull. "Think just because you got a little tit, you're a big fuckin' lover. Well, I hope you do get laid. It'll be the first time."

The only thing I was about ready to do was blackout from David's scissor-lock. I gripped his ankles as tightly as I could and shoved upward, as if I was trying to break the world bench press record. It worked. I snapped my head loose and spun away. Both of us sprang to our feet at the same time, but I was a split second faster and landed a roundhouse right cross flush on David's jaw. The lucky punch in the dark sent him sprawling backwards against the chest and down hard onto the floor on his butt. I stood there in the darkness with my fists ready for more. David didn't say anything. He just sat there leaning against the chest. I could just make out Big Red's silhouette, as he hurried over to David and nervously licked his face...

...After about ten-thousand pillow fights, that began when I was about three, I'd learned not to trust David all that much. He'd played possum and outfoxed me too many times. Once, I think I was six and sleeping over at his house, we were really going at it in David's upstairs bedroom. I seemed to have had the upper hand and was getting in more pillow-hits, when David feigned exhaustion and collapsed onto his bed. I, naturally, didn't take advantage of the situation and flopped onto the guest bed, which was considered mine because no one else ever used it except me. Anyway, I was laughing and catching my breath at the same time; when, suddenly, everything went dark and I couldn't breathe. David had pounced on top of me and was smothering my face with his pillow. Of course, he really didn't smother me for long; but, at the time, it truly frightened me – as I'm quite sure he'd meant it to...

So, there I stood, in the middle of a dark bedroom in David's family's summer cottage, on the uppermost reaches of the northern coast of Maine, waiting for his next move. I didn't have to wait long. But, it was not what I had expected. Not by a long shot. David slowly got up, brushed by me, shoved the mattress onto his bed and got into his sleeping bag. I stood there in the dark for another moment, and then got back into my own sleeping bag. Big Red came over and gave my cheek a couple of swift licks, circled several times on the braided rug, and flopped down for the night. Glad the fight was over. So was I.

"Fuck you," David said quietly. He had succeeded in getting in the last face-saving shot with his favorite word-weapon.

For as long as I could remember, I don't think David and I had ever been in a real fist fight before. I mean, actually trying to inflict pain and injury on one another. Although, I had sometimes suspected that David had gone right to the edge with me, when we'd had some heated arguments along the way, but we'd never had an honest-to-goodness fist fight. Something was definitely changing.

We had only been in Maine for one full day and already we'd met up with the local dimwitted tour guide, who was either a brother, cousin or... probably even sister... for all I knew, to everyone in the town. I'd had the shit scared out of me by the creature from the back of the general store. David had taken me deep into the 'virgin forest' and explained how the demented locals toss their inbred deformed babies off the cliff-of-death. We'd performed a surprise attack on the skunk outpost and been repelled with gas warfare. I'd come face-to-face with the 'demon-dog-from-hell' and been forced to take a shower with vinegar. David had shown me how to skewer a naked 'bird' with a cattail. And, to top it off, the best looking girl on that remote asteroid had chosen me as a pawn to piss off her evil kinda-boyfriend. I had failed square dancing. Crashed into a brook. And, just because a girl named Sandy had large breasts and let me feel one of them, I'd hit my best friend in the face.

I laid my head back on the pillow and stared up into the darkness... then, closed my eyes.

NINE

THE SCREAMING PLACE

...Sandy... I was supposed to meet Sandy at the store at ten o'clock tomorrow... *Patricia... Patricia* wouldn't be there. She'd run out of the Orpheum Theater because I was sitting next to another girl. I'd never even gotten a chance to tell her I liked her... I would... I would take care of that as soon... as soon as... that sound... popping gum?... Slap... Slap... It came from somewhere far away... the brook... It came from the brook... The black-and-white demon guy. It was almost dark and I was supposed to be home. I had to leave... *the frog!...the frog!...* Slap...Slap... That awful sound. It wouldn't go away... Slap-slap-slap-slap... Slap-slap-slap-slap...

I sat straight up in my sleeping bag. It was daylight. I was in the bedroom in Maine on one of the twin beds. Big Red was sitting right next to me. His tail was slapping hard and happily on the hardwood floor. I blinked my eyes and shook my head completely awake. I was alive and still fifteen-and-a-half years old.

The smell of bacon and eggs cooking drew me into the kitchen. The small breakfast table was set for two and David was at the stove. Cooking. I couldn't believe it. David was actually cooking breakfast for us. He looked over at me standing in the doorway in my undershorts and grinned like nothing had happened. "Hey, look who's up and looks like shit," he said cheerily. I noticed that his left cheek was very red.

"Listen, no hard feelings, huh? It's better I'm with Mildred anyway," David said and scooped the well-done scrambled eggs and almost blackened bacon onto two plates and set them unceremoniously on the table. He continued to chatter on, "I mean, the way I see it, I can really help'er into the millennium."

I sat at the table and looked at the singed pile of brownish-yellow eggs and extra-extra crispy bacon swimming in a pool of grease. I knew I had to eat it. How could I hurt my best friend's feelings, after having aced him out of the local beauty queen and punched his lights out.

David sat down opposite me and started gobbling down the gourmet entree while he rattled on at the same time. "Ya-see, if I'd've ended up with Sandy, poor little Mildred probably never would've gotten her cherry broken." Leave it to David to come up with that one. "Now," he continued and started laughing through a mouthful of greasy eggs, "she'll know what it's like to be boffed by someone who really knows how it's done, instead of by one of these jerk stump-fuckers up here. I'll just consider it my little contribution to the underprivileged."

I looked at the eggs I hadn't touched. "Hey, man, eat up," David said with his patented leer. "You're gonna need all the stamina you can get or Sandy'll think she picked the wrong guy."

Shit. Got me again. Suddenly, I wasn't hungry.

We let Big Red ride into town with us. "How long're you gonna be?" David asked as he wheeled the station wagon away from the cottage and gunned it down the wooded road.

"I dunno," I mumbled. Maybe she wouldn't show up. Maybe, her kinda-boyfriend threw her off the cliff and David and Big Red and I could go fishing.

David pulled up in front of the general store. There wasn't a soul in sight. The entire street was deserted. Not even the town's devil-dog mascot was lurking in the alley next to the store, ready to leap at me and tear my throat out with his rabies-dripping fangs.

"Looks like you've been stood up, lover-boy," David advised me, with more than an inference of satisfaction.

"We're early," I replied, trying to hide my relief.

"Hey, I almost forgot. I gotta get me some rubbers. These hicky chicks up here are probably Petri dishes for every STD they make."

David got out of the car and leaned back through the opened window. "You want any?" he asked with his leer.

"No."

"You better, man. The only pill they ever heard of up here is aspirin. I'll get you some anyway." Before I could protest, David had leaped up onto the wooden sidewalk and disappeared into the store.

I sat in the car waiting. Except for Big Red panting patiently in the back of the station wagon, it was pretty quiet. Then, I heard the rumble of a car coming and looked up the street. It wasn't a car. It was a battered pickup truck and it was heading toward the general store.

It parked right next to me. Sandy was driving and she was alone.

"Hi," she said with a bright smile on her face.

"Hi," I returned. My face beeting red.

"Fancy meetin' you here."

"Yeah..."

"Wanna go for a ride?"

My heart leaped into my throat and sat on my vocal cords. "Sure," I croaked.

I got out of the station wagon and started around to the passenger side of the pickup. "You drive," Sandy said and slid over on the seat to make room for me behind the wheel.

I was really stuck. I couldn't make a dumb excuse like I didn't have a license. Without his mother knowing it, I'd been driving David's station wagon with him for over three months and, as David said, there wasn't any law to speak of around this part of the state. "Oh...right...Yeah-right," I fumbled and started back toward the driver's side, just as David came out of the store.

"Hey, Billy-boy," he called and came up to me.

"Yeah?"

David gripped my arm and steered me away from the pickup truck. "You can have'im in a minute," he called to Sandy over his shoulder. Then, he huddled in close and spoke in a conspiratorial whisper, "Listen, there's no sense in bein' mad, right?"

"I'm not mad," I whispered back.

David gave a quick glance back at Sandy and shielded me from her view. Then, he offered me his hand. "Shake on it," he ordered.

I shook his hand and immediately felt something

odd being pressed into my palm. David squeezed my hand tighter. I looked at him. His face was inches from mine and he had a peculiar grin that gave me a strange feeling inside. Then, David let go of my hand. I looked down at the small package of foil-wrapped condoms he'd passed to me and felt myself flush red. I quickly shoved the package into my jeans and glanced over at Sandy sitting several yards away in the pickup truck. She smiled, but I didn't think she saw the packet of rubbers.

"Have fun," David whispered devilishly.

"I...I gotta go," I muttered.

"Yeah, me too. I gotta get old Mildred in the saddle," David said, still whispering and still trying to save face and one-up me. I turned to leave. David stopped me and spoke in his best hushed, authoritative tone, "Better not let that pus-brain Ira see you with her."

I looked at him, wondering what he was really saying. With David, you never knew. Sometimes he meant just the opposite of what he said. For a split second, I had a strange feeling that he might just want Ira to see me with Sandy and beat the living shit out of me. But, I quickly rejected the thought as too merciless, even for David.

As I walked toward the pickup truck, I glanced over my shoulder at David. He gave me a little shrug and a grin, and then said, "Hey, don't do anything I wouldn't do."

I climbed up into the pickup beside Sandy, who immediately moved over close to me. As I started the truck, I saw David get into the station wagon. A dark expression had replaced his grin. Big Red was looking quizzically at me through the back window. The wag in his tail was slow and seemed a little unsure. So was I.

David gunned the station wagon in a squealing U-turn and roared back up the road toward the cottage. As he disappeared around the far turn and into the woods at the end of town, the sharp report of a 'backfire' ricocheted through the trees. It sounded just like a gunshot. David saying "fuck you" once again.

"Is everything alright?" Sandy asked.

"Yeah," I answered hesitantly, trying to convince myself, "everything's fine."

I followed Sandy's directions and drove the pickup along a quiet back road that wandered lazily up the side of a pine-studded mountain. The air was crystal clear and warm. The higher we went the more picturesque the scenery became. As the forest thinned out, it gave way to sloping open spaces that were dotted with protruding glacier rocks surrounded by knee-high grass and summer wildflowers. I thought of Big Red and how he loved to bound through our fields of wildflowers back home after gigantic butterflies. The farther we drove, the further behind I was able to leave what had taken place during the past twenty-four hours. David would've told me something about the brain being an amazing instrument that's able to block and filter out different packages of information at different times to accommodate the situation at hand. He was always spouting off about heady stuff like that, ever since he discovered that 'fuck' was much more than a four-letter word.

I guess I must have driven about five or ten miles up the mountain before I realized that Sandy and I hadn't spoken to each other, since I first got behind the wheel and drove out of town. I looked over at Sandy seated right next to me. Although I hadn't noticed it, she had actually moved right up against me. There was something about her that seemed very different from when I first met her at the barn dance. She seemed softer and much prettier. It was hard to believe she could be related to Petey.

I could also see that she wasn't wearing all that much either. Just some thin white cotton shorts and a kind of red checkered halter top that barely covered her breasts. To control any embarrassing feelings that might arise, I forced myself to concentrate on maneuvering the truck around the narrow bends in the road. As we zigzagged slowly up the mountain, Sandy must have sensed that my blood was beginning to surge a little, because she broke the silence. "That was kinda scary last night. I'm sure glad no one got hurt," she said.

I could feel her looking at me. In fact, I'd felt her eyes on me ever since we drove out of town. "Me, too," I answered stiffly. "How's Mildred?"

"She'll be okay. She's just gonna stay in bed today."

...Stay in bed? I thought David said he was gonna...

"Is that guy your boyfriend?" I asked much too abruptly, as I wheeled around a sharp turn in the road. Sandy didn't answer me. The road straightened out, so I was able to glance over at her. She was staring straight ahead and had a very disturbing, dark expression on her face, almost a look of revulsion.

Finally, she answered in a soft unemotional tone, "No, he's not my...my boyfriend."

I gulped a bit, wondering if I should really pursue the point. But, after what Petey had said about 'best not' and David telling me not to let Ira catch me with her, I just muttered, "He sure was mad."

Sandy waited a long moment, before she spoke,

then sighed, "We split up two months ago."

"Oh."

Sandy indicated a narrow dirt road up ahead, which shot off between a thin cropping of pine and birch trees to the left. I slowed down and turned onto what was more of a rutted pathway. "Where're we going?" I asked as the truck bumped over the deep ruts. I could hardly see ahead of us. Tree branches had grown down over the road that obviously hadn't been used in years.

"Just a little secret place of mine," she answered in a soft, sweet voice.

I looked at Sandy sitting right next to me. The dark cloud had disappeared. Her smiling brown eyes sparkled as she looked at me. There was an air of anticipation coming from her that I couldn't explain. All I knew was that my entire body began to feel warm all over. "How far?" I asked a little hoarsely.

"Just a little ways more."

Suddenly, the narrow dirt roadway came to an abrupt end. The trees opened up to a spectacular blanket of white daisies that rolled over an expansive clearing, surrounded by a solid ring of white birch trees. "Stop here," Sandy said. I stopped the truck and shut the engine off. It was an amazing sight. Nothing but white like a first snow. Birds chirped in the trees and tiny butterflies fluttered from flower to flower.

"Come on," Sandy said excitedly as she opened her door and jumped out of the truck.

Through the windshield, I watched her run through the white flowers toward a large boulder that jutted up out of the sea of daisies like a giant gray whale exploding through the surface of the ocean. She got to the base of the big ten foot rock and, without looking back, scrambled to the top. "Hurry," she shouted to me.

I got out of the truck and followed her path through the daisies to the rock and climbed up beside her. Her dark eyes were dancing with excitement. "Isn't it great!" she exclaimed. "You can see for a million miles." And, you could. From where we stood together, on top of the whale's nose, the sea of daisies sloped gently down and away. We could see over the birch trees, over the sweeping green forests to a far off range of mountains, and beyond to the infinite horizon.

"Yeah, it's great," I replied, completely swept away by the vista set out before us.

Sandy paused for a moment, then looked up at me. "This is my screamin' place," she said with a shyness I hadn't heard before. Her face seemed almost radiant in the bright sun. I began to feel lightheaded. Maybe it was the altitude, I thought.

"Your what?" I asked.

She looked at me with that searching look again. "Haven't...haven't you ever wanted to scream? Just go someplace where nobody is and..." She stopped. She kept searching my eyes. Looking for something. Her voice became almost a whisper, as she continued, "...scream your head off?"

'Well, I..." was all I could say.

Then suddenly, Sandy put her hands to her face and her eyes danced as she spoke. "It's great. When everythin' gets all mixed-up inside me, I come up here an' just scream until I can't scream no more." Her eyes seemed to desperately want me to understand.

"Really?" I said. I tried not to sound too astounded

at the thought of standing on top of a rock that looked like Jonah-the-whale, screaming my fool head off in the middle of nowhere, with some girl I'd barely met and French kissed, and felt up, and pissed off her kinda-boyfriend, and punched out my best friend over. And, I had a pocket full of rubbers, too.

"Yeah," Sandy said enthusiastically. Then, she offered me a challenge that almost sent me tripping off the rock. "Try it."

"Huh?"

"Come on, it's really great."

The beets were back on my face. "Nah, I don't..."

The long piercing scream, that she suddenly emitted, took me completely by surprise. She stopped and looked at me. I could see the exhilaration in her face. "See? Go ahead. Try one."

I grinned, feeling very sheepish inside, but at the same time, tempted to try at least one little scream for the hell of it. But, my head shook a "no" instead. What the hell was I doing there?

"Go ahead, Billy," she urged. "Go ahead and do it."

I hesitated, and then let out a halfhearted little "yelp" that wouldn't have come anywhere near to solving the things that I was mixed-up about; especially, all the new things that had begun to swirl around inside my head that I didn't understand.

"No-no. That won't do it," she scolded with a smile. "Come on. Like this." With that, Sandy threw her head back and let out a bloodcurdling scream that was so loud and piercing that a flock of birds flushed out of some nearby birch trees, swooped down and veered sharply off away from the clearing. I stared at her, astonished that such a shriek could come from anyone, let alone someone as small as Sandy. She didn't stop. She kept right on screaming. Louder and louder.

I don't know when I joined in screaming right along with her; but all of a sudden, I felt an incredible surge of energy, something different and exhilarating that I couldn't remember ever feeling before. Sandy grabbed my hand and we held on tightly to each other, atop the tip of the whale's nose, in the middle of an ocean of flowing white daisies, screaming our fool heads off.

Mine were short screams at first. Then, as Sandy's grew louder, so did mine. Our coinciding screams reverberated through the surrounding circle of birch trees and echoed down over the green forests, where they lapped up against the far-off mountain range and evaporated into the horizon. I saw a deer, a large doe, jump into our white daisy covered screaming place, its eyes wide with startled confusion, its body frozen in place, its head locked on us as we straddled the top of the whale rock. Its large brown ears twitched nervously, until the animal abruptly turned and bounded back to safety among the trees. A gray rabbit darted up the path we'd made through the snow white daisy blanket, stopped short, and skittered back where it'd come from.

Sandy reached way down into herself and let go with a gut-wrenching wail. I found myself wanting to outdo her and reached down further, throwing my entire body into a scream to the heavens above that took me right down to my knees. Black-and-white blotches flashed in front of my eyes. I couldn't stand up and landed on all fours. Sandy grabbed me around my waist. I started slipping off the whale's nose. She held onto me, our bodies heaving violently together, gasping and shivering in near collapse.

Then, slowly, we regained our strength. I pushed myself up onto my feet and pulled Sandy up beside me. Her face was flushed and streaming with perspiration. I could feel my own sweat running down my face. She smiled up at me. I smiled back. I'd done something with someone that I'd never done with anyone else before. Not even David. It was almost like getting drunk only better.

We were still breathing hard, as Sandy stepped in front of me and leaned back against my chest. She reached back and eased my arms around in front of her, holding them firmly with her own... up under her breasts. I could feel her heart beating hard against my forearm.

"Wasn't' it great?" she said between breaths.

"Yeah," I managed to get out. She seemed to be easing my arms up higher on her body - over her red checkered halter top - over her large breasts.

"It really gets all the junk out of you," she said in a breathy whisper.

I could feel the heat rising inside of me and felt lightheaded again. Slowly, Sandy turned around within my arms and faced me, pressing her body into mine. Her eyes closed halfway. Her lips parted. "Kiss me," she murmured.

I obeyed. We kissed long and hungrily. I'd never kissed anyone like that before. I didn't even know if what I was feeling was supposed to be what I was feeling like. All I knew was that I was getting on the 'roller coaster' again. Sandy pulled her lips away from mine. Her eyes were transfixed. She didn't say a word, as she took my hand and slowly started backing down off the rock.

We stood there for a moment, at the base of the

whale, knee-deep in white daisies. Looking at each other. Not speaking. Without taking her eyes off of mine, Sandy knelt into the flowers and drew me down beside her. Then, she let go of my hand and eased herself down on her back. There was a strange, almost hypnotic look in her half-closed eyes. I'd seen David get it once. Where? I couldn't stop my mind from spinning around. I couldn't get off the roller coaster... *at the brook...at the brook...* I bent my body awkwardly down over hers and kissed her warm, soft lips for what seemed like a long time... *the frog!...the frog!*

I felt her hand ease under my chest and lightly press against me. I sat back. She sat up in front of me. Her eyes were still on mine - half closed. Her lips parted. I didn't move. I couldn't. She reached out and lifted my sweat drenched tee-shirt over my head, exposing my bare chest to her. My heart pounded in my ears, as her fingers drifted lightly down over my shoulders and through the dark hair that had recently begun to grow on my chest. Then, she withdrew her hand and reached up behind her neck and untied her red checkered halter top, letting it fall to her waist. Her breasts were round and pink. Not at all like all the photographs of the overdeveloped women in David's secret collection of big boob magazines. Sandy let me look at her for a long moment, then quietly removed her red checkered halter top and set it down on the white daisies beside her.

My mind began to race out of control... It must have been shortly after David had taught me things that summer, behind the bush at the river, that I'd started trying to imagine what it would be like to be with a girl...

Sandy slid her white shorts down over her bare legs. I could feel my hands begin to shake, as she lay back down on the bed of white daisies and waited for me. "Billy," she breathed.

...Almost every night from that day on, I'd fall asleep thinking about the strange, wonderful, and secret feelings I possessed; and how I would try to hide the evidence from my mother in the morning, when I'd wake up to discover that I had made a mistake during the night...

"Billy," she murmured again and held her hands out to me.

...My mother never let on if she knew what I was doing or not... My mother... Oh-my-God!... The roller coaster spun out of control and left the tracks...

I groped for my belt. I wasn't wearing one. My shaking fingers fumbled with my fly and I managed to slide my jeans down, before I realized I couldn't get them over my shoes. Sandy lay there quietly and watched me undress.

...The roller coaster sailed through the open sky... Over the clouds... Up into the blue... Someone else was sitting next to me in the front seat. The black-and-white demon...

Sandy's arms wrapped around my back. She was soft, so soft. "It's okay, Billy. Let me. It's okay."

...The roller coaster...it... I couldn't stop it. Faster and faster...

"Yes, Billy! Yes!"

...I couldn't stop the roller coaster. I grabbed and held on for dear life. I was going to...to...

"Let it go, Billy. Let it go inside of me."

...I wasn't using the rubbers David bought for me... What if she gets pregnant? Oh-my-God! The roller coaster roared straight up into the sky, then whip-snapped around and plummeted back down...down...down...toward the white circle of snow white daisies... *Where's Patricia? Where did Patricia go?* She ran out of the Orpheum Theater because I was sitting next to one of David's friends. I had to go after her. I had to find her and tell her it wasn't what she'd thought. It wasn't my fault! But, it was dark outside the theater and Patricia was gone...

"It's alright, Billy," Sandy murmured in my ear, "don't cry. It's alright. It was wonderful." I felt her hand patting my hair. I could smell her body. I could feel myself inside of her. I could feel the tears in my own eyes. She kissed me softly on my cheek, then placed her hands on my face and eased my head up from her chest. Her eyes were sparkling as she smiled up at me. "You were wonderful, Billy." I let go of the two clumps of white daisies I had jerked from the ground and crushed in my hands.

For the first few miles we didn't speak at all, as I drove the battered pickup truck back down the mountain. It was just as well, because I wasn't sure if I was still inside the body that was driving the truck. Everything seemed as light as air - my arms - my legs - my entire body felt as if it was floating all around me. I looked over at Sandy. Her head was resting back on the seat. Her eyes were closed. Perspiration had dampened the dark brown hair that framed her face with small, shiny wet curls. She was smiling peacefully. I felt her hand resting easily on my thigh. The drive back down the mountain seemed to take much longer.

"Billy."

Hearing her murmur my name startled me. I gripped the steering wheel tighter. "Yeah."

She paused, then said quietly, "You're not like..."

I waited, but she'd stopped. I glanced over at her. Her head was still resting back on the seat and her eyes were still closed. But, her smile was gone. "Like what?" I asked.

"Like...like anyone I've ever known."

I gripped the steering wheel even tighter. All of a sudden, the mountain road seemed incredibly narrow and I was sure that, if I didn't concentrate, I would miss a curve and drive right off a cliff.

Sandy lifted her head and I felt her hand tighten a little on my leg. "How do you feel?" she asked.

The recurring dry spot reoccurred in my throat as I answered, "Fine."

"I mean, about me."

"I guess...I guess I feel...different."

Her hand tightened on my jeans again. "Was it your first time?"

My ego jumped in, trying to rescue itself. "No."

She giggled and squeezed my leg. "Yes, it was."

"Are you laughing at me?" I asked. Beet red.

Sandy grabbed my arm and I almost hit the soft shoulder going around a curve. "No-no, Billy, I'm not laughing at you. Honest, I'm not. I'm just glad it..." She stopped again.

"What?" I asked.

She let go of my arm and looked away. Her hands were clasped together in her lap. I didn't know what else to ask or say and I guessed she didn't either. We had almost reached the base of the mountain. "I'm just glad it was with me," she whispered in such a hushed voice that I wasn't sure at first what she'd said. But, as we drove back through the town and turned onto the road back up to the cottage, her words came into my head very clearly. *...I'm just glad it was with me...*

I drove slowly up to the cottage and parked several yards away from David's station wagon. We were both quiet for a moment. I could tell that Sandy didn't want me to leave yet, so I just waited and looked through the bug-splattered windshield of the truck at the tall pines that circled the cottage.

"Billy?" she asked softly.

"Yeah?"

"Do...do you..." She hesitated.

"What?" I asked.

She looked straight ahead and clutched her hands tightly together in her lap. Finally, she looked right at me and asked in a soft, firm voice, "Do you think you could ever love someone like me?"

The feeling hit me like a shot. Love? Thoughts raced through my head like someone pulling hard on a string top. Love? Was that what it was? I looked over at the girl sitting beside me. I had been with her. I had been 'inside' her. I had really and truly made love to her. "Yes," I said with a slight croak in my throat.

Sandy's face glistened in the late afternoon sunlight that sifted through the pine trees. I could feel my own eyes glazing over. Sandy touched my arm and came closer. She kissed me slowly - for a long time. Then, she pulled away and sat next to her door, leaving a space between us. She looked over at the clean, white cottage for a moment, and then asked, "How far do you live from here?"

"Um...almost four hundred miles, why?"

"Oh, nothin'."

I saw a flicker of what looked like hurt in her eyes, as she gazed straight ahead again. "I..." she started, "...I've never even been to the next town but once. I...I wouldn't know how to even act around city people." She sighed and stared up at the roof of the truck. "Someday, I'd sure like to go an' see the capital of Augusta, just to see what it's like." Then, wistfully, "Someday."

"Why don't you go?"

Sandy reached up and picked absently at the tattered, brownish lining that covered most of the rusted metal. "Well, when some of the boys around here burnt down the schoolhouse and ran the teacher out of town, I was only in the fifth grade. Problem was the nearest other school is more than forty miles away, too far for most of us up here. So, that's all the school I've ever been to." She took a small piece of the roof lining down to her lap and began to rub it together between her fingertips. "They keep sayin' they're gonna build us another one, but they never seem to get around to it." The little piece of rotten roof lining disintegrated into dust. "I just wouldn't know what to do when I got there."

"Sure you would," I said, trying to reassure her.

Her eyes began to glisten. "Billy?" she asked very quietly.

"Yeah?"

She measured her words as she spoke. Her voice was very uncertain, as if she already knew the answer to her question. "Do...do you think I could ever come visit you? I mean, if..."

"Sure," I said right over her, "sure you can." My

heart gave a thump against the inside of my chest, like a large air bubble had passed right through it.

"Do you have a father?" she asked.

"Of course," I answered, a little taken aback.

She looked up and started picking at the roof lining again. "Mine's gone away."

"Oh."

"I mean, he never come back through here after he was with my mother that one time. I've never seen him."

"But, I heard you say..."

"Oh, my mother has a man we call Pa, but he's not mine."

Sandy didn't look down from the roof for a long moment. Then, when she did, she looked over at me with a very distant, almost isolated expression. "I really like you, Billy...I..."

Without thinking I took the initiative, slid over next to her, and kissed her like we'd kissed on top of the mountain... *I'm just glad it was with me...*

I opened the door, got out and stood beside the truck, sort of alternately looking off at the trees and down at my shoes. Sandy slid quietly behind the wheel. Neither of us spoke, until she calmly uttered, "I really like you, Billy." I looked at her through the open truck window. The smile she had on her face reminded me, in some strange way, of how my mother had sometimes smiled at me, as if she'd instinctively understood my confusion. It made me feel both warm and somewhat empty at the same time.

"There's a carnival tonight," Sandy said, "wanna go?"

"Sure, where is it?"

From where I was standing, I couldn't see what Sandy saw, as she glanced over at the cottage before she answered me. "Petey knows," she said quietly, her mood darkening.

"What time?"

"Anytime, I'll be there."

I smiled at her and would've kissed her again had she not started the truck's engine. "Great," I said, "I'll be there, too."

Sandy looked at me for a moment, then reached out and gently touched my cheek with her fingertips. "Come'ere," she said softly. I stepped to the window. She kissed me very tenderly; then, without another word, drove away from the cottage and on down the dirt drive.

The sun was gently slipping down behind the tall pine trees. I stood there alone in the quiet of the surrounding forest. As I absently put my hands into my jeans, I felt the foil-wrapped packet that David had given me crammed down inside my right pocket. Something drew my eyes over to the front window of the cottage. The skinny figure of Petey Peak was standing just behind the left curtain looking out at me. I knew, then, what Sandy had seen when she'd looked over at the cottage. "Petey knows." Petey had probably been watching us the whole time we'd been parked there. Somehow, I didn't care what he'd seen and walked across the gravel parking circle toward the front door.

As the late afternoon sun eased out of sight, a whisper of a breeze began to filter through the thick pine boughs, bringing an end to my second day in Maine.

TEN

SECRETS

Big Red met me at the door, leaped up, set his paws on my chest and licked my face excitedly. Then, as I entered the living room, Big Red circumvented Petey who was slumped in a chair with a beer, pretending he hadn't been watching Sandy and me through the window. I didn't blame Big Red for being rude; Petey was another matter, sitting there wearing his usual body cologne.

David was sprawled on the couch snoring with his mouth open. A small pyramid of empty beer cans was stacked beside him on the food-littered coffee table, along with a couple of David's old standby big boob magazines that he had stashed at the cottage a few years back.

"What's with him?" I asked Petey dryly.

Petey squinted at me with his little pellet eyes and picked at the residents living on his scalp. "Sleepin'," he muttered.

I could see that and went over and shook David's foot. "Hey, David, wake up." David stirred, then groaned and rolled over on the couch so his back was to me. "Are you drunk?" I asked. He didn't answer, so I shook him by his shoulder. "Come on, get up."

David turned his head and blinked his eyes open. He took a moment to focus, and then shot me a sarcastic sneer. "Well, look who's back. The great fuckin' lover boy himself."

"Screw off," I muttered and turned toward the kitchen. I hadn't eaten all day and didn't feel like messing around with David's bullshit.

"Well?" David taunted and sat up.

I stopped and turned around, knowing full well that David had no intention of letting me off the hook, until he was satisfied that I'd given him every gory detail of my day with Sandy. I wasn't about to. "Well, what?" I snapped back at him.

"Well?" he pursued with new intensity.

I could feel my blood rapidly rising into my face. "Hey, I thought you were gonna lay off."

"Oh, cool it, will'ya," he said, brushing it off. "I'm just pissed that's all. Fuckin' Mildred didn't show, so Petey and I went fishing." Then, he ordered me to, "Get us a beer." He turned to Petey. "You want a beer, Petey?" Petey shrugged.

"Get your own beer," I said.

David heaved a long, dramatic sigh and stood up. As he headed for the kitchen, he mumbled to me out of the side of his mouth, "I got somethin' to tell you."

David went into the kitchen. I turned to Petey. "What's he talking about?" Petey gave me a shrug and looked away. I called to David in the kitchen, "What're you talking about?"

David came back into the living room with three beers and tossed one to Petey and one to me. "You better sit down," he ordered me.

"Why?" I answered and stood my ground.

He glared at me. "Sit down, goddammit!" David's sharp tone said that something might really be up. I sat in an easy chair next to the coffee table. David snapped open his beer and sat at the end of the couch nearest to me. He looked over at Petey, who had slouched down further into his chair so that his chin was on his chest. His little raisin eyes looked directly at me.

David took a big gulp of his beer, swallowed, and then waited a moment before he spoke. David was always big on waiting a moment before he had something he thought was profound to say. He set his can of beer onto the coffee table and moved over closer to me. "Listen," he started with, "messing around with Sandy is gonna..."

My defensive mechanism interrupted David's flow. “It’s none of your business.”

"Okay-okay, it doesn't matter. She's gonna get us in a shit-load of trouble.”

"Oh, come off it."

David folded his hands on his knees and leaned forward, never a good sign. It was always an indication that he really meant business. "She's really bad news. You better listen."

All of a sudden I felt a sense of panic in my stomach, like David was going to drop some bomb on me. I was right.

"Ira Peak showed up here this morning."

I didn't respond right away. My eyes shifted across the room. Petey was still drilling me. Not even blinking. "So?" I finally asked dry-throated.

"So," David repeated, raising his voice. "He was lookin' for you. That's so!"

My heart fibrillated noticeably. I remembered how Ira's fierce black eyes had dilated when he'd glared at David, who was just trying to thank him for pulling the station wagon out of the creek. "What...what'd he want?" I asked, trying to hide the shudder that rippled through my body.

David leaned back and stretched his arms along the top of the couch. There was a smug look on his face that he got whenever he knew he was playing with a stacked deck. Then, he announced, "He knew you were out with Sandy."

I would have understood his self-righteous attitude, if he was just pissed off that I'd gotten to Sandy first. But that same feeling hit me again; that somehow, David really wanted Ira Peak to kick the shit out of me. "Big deal," I said to him, trying to muster up as much bravado as I could - and not believing it for a minute.

As quickly as a mercury thermometer, David's temper began to heat up. He looked at me, squinting his eyes for effect. "Well, he's just a little pissed off that someone is out dicking around with..." he stopped and glanced over at Petey, then looked back at me,"...with his wife."

I couldn't believe my ears. I mean, that was even too far-fetched for David to come up with. "His...his wife," I uttered. The pressure roared into my brain.

"That's right."

"...But...they're not..." I glanced nervously at Petey then back at David. "They split up or something."

"Oh," David announced sarcastically, "I see you two really did get to know each other."

I stood up. I'd just about had it with David. My face was probably beet red but I didn't care. "That's right, mouth," I shouted at him, "and, I'll tell you something else." I couldn't believe what I was about to say, but I couldn't stop myself either. "I...I think I'm in love with her."

David didn't move. He just stared at me with no expression at all. Petey stopped in mid-drink and focused his surprised pin-hole eyes on me. Even Big Red's head popped up from where he was curled up on the braided rug. Finally, David muttered through the stunned silence in the room, "You're what?"

"You heard me," I answered, defiantly.

"Jesus Christ, you're fuckin' crazy."

"You don’t know anything about her,” I shouted back.

"What the hell're you gonna do, take'er back home with you?"

Even though I somehow knew it couldn't be me doing my talking, I went on because of the strange new powerful feeling swelling inside me that I was unable to control. "Maybe," I shot back at David. "Maybe, I will!"

David jumped up from the couch. "Oh, God, you can’t be serious," he shouted at the ceiling. "You’re gonna bring’er home with us? Where’s she gonna live...with your parents?”

"Knock it off, David," I shouted back. I was really getting mad. Big Red was up on his feet, pacing nervously.

"Listen," David said, "I better tell you some things about that girl besides her already being married."

"She's not married."

David held up his hand and restrained himself. "I know-I know... Okay..." He heaved an exasperated sigh, and then went on, "It’s not like how we get married. You remember me telling you things are different up here?"

"Yeah-yeah, a million times."

The concerned expression in David's eyes was getting to me. Although, he made it sound real enough, I couldn't get rid of the feeling that it might be just another one of David's overly clever stories he'd dreamed up to get his way. That was always the problem with David. I could never really tell for sure, because he was so good at always making everything look and sound so real.

"Well," he began, "they are different. That girl you think you're in love with is more than Ira Peak's wife." The bomb I thought was the bomb wasn't the bomb. It was only a firecracker compared to the real bomb David laid on me. "She's his cousin."

I stood there. My knees felt weak. Petey hadn't moved from his slouched position in the chair. His expressionless little snake eyes were staring right at me. I waited a moment. All eyes were on me. Petey's... David's... and Big Red's. "So, what?" was all I could come up with.

David glanced over at Petey, then back at me. "First cousins," he said in a flat voice, letting his latest bombshell lay there for dramatic effect. "And, there's no such thing up here as being married or divorced." I didn't say anything. David had become such a goddamned liar. Why would he lie to me? *...Just because I was the one who...* David continued with his wealth of information on the habits of the local citizenry. "That's because up here a guy just claims a girl for himself and makes it with'er." *...Liar...* "And, if they decide to live together, that means they're married." *...Jesus Christ. What a fucking liar. No wonder I'd punched him...*

"Well," I gritted, trying to hold my temper in, "where I come from, she's not married."

"Jesus, Billy. Come on, will-ya? This isn't like the

nice little town we live in. This is the edge of the fucking world."

"Oh, shit," I scoffed at his drama.

David sat on the edge of the couch and pointed right at Petey. "See that guy over there? Well, he can't even read or write." He turned to Petey. "Can you, Petey?" Petey just looked into the opening in his can of beer. David quickly honed in on me, trying to drive his point home. "And, you know why? Because, ten years ago they ran the teacher out of town and burned down the fucking school."

"I know all about that." I wasn't about to cave. David was good, but this was really getting absurd. "Besides, what's that got to do with Sandy?" I countered.

David gave Petey a quick glance, then stood up and motioned me toward the front door. "Come on outside," he ordered.

"Why?" I asked, just as he opened the door.

"I've got something private to say."

David walked outside. I stood there in the small living room. Thoughts collided in my head. Why should I buy into his bullshit? It was all just a made-up story because he was pissed off at me for going out with Sandy. I mean, what was one girl to him anyway? He was always bragging about nailing all those girls from Vic's back home. What was so important about Sandy that he had to get all bent out of shape?

I followed him outside over toward the woods. David and I stood face-to-face beside the station wagon. I couldn't believe what he had just said. "What kid? What're you talking about? She doesn't have a kid."

"How do you know?" David asked me, almost

shouting right in my face.

"How do you know?" I shouted right back. I heard Big Red whining at the window, but didn't look around.

"I don't. But, she could have," David answered.

I threw up my hands and spun around in a full circle of exasperation. "God, what're you talking about? You're such a liar, David."

"Really? Oh, really? Do I have to spell it out for you?" David fired back. Then he did something that truly annoyed me. He jabbed me in my chest with his index finger, a jab for each word. "She's-one-of-them," he jabbed.

I grabbed his finger and bent it back away from me. "Don't give me that 'virgin forest' bullshit again."

David backed off and walked out in front of the station wagon. His back was to me. "Billy," he began after a moment, "she's just as crazy as the rest of these brain-dead freaks up here."

"She's not. She's different."

He turned around. "She's different alright. She's just lookin' for someone to get'er out of here, that's all. Anyone."

"Bullshit!" I said right at him.

"Okay. Why do you think Percy keeps hangin' around, huh? Because, he wants me to take him back with me. And, you wanna know somethin'?"

"What?"

David stepped closer. "If I said I would take him outta here, he wouldn't go."

"Why not?"

"Because, he knows he doesn't know how to do anything and he knows he's different from normal people.

He's never even seen a fuckin' train." I just looked at David for a second, then over at Big Red, who had his paws up on the windowsill, staring out at us. "An' you know what else?" David asked in a curious tone that told me he had another one of his little bombs to drop. I just looked at him without saying anything. A smirk appeared on his face. "Mildred's got a dick," he announced with a shit-eating grin.

I actually stepped backwards. "What!" I uttered incredulously.

"No shit," David continued excitedly. "Petey says she was born with a fuckin' dick and a..."

"Goddammit, David," I shouted over him. "You're the one who's brain-dead." I turned away, completely disgusted with David and all of his bullshit stories.

"No-wait, she's one of those hermaphrodites!" he gleefully exclaimed and started laughing. "She...she can get laid and jerk off at the same time."

I couldn't stand it anymore and blew up at him. "If this is such a freaked-out place, why the hell did we come up here?"

David stopped and looked at me for a moment. He probably thought I was ready to punch him out again. I don't think it would've taken much. Then, his quirky, sardonic smile crossed his face. "Because," he started evenly, "I thought we could just screw around and have a little fun with the locals." He stopped again. A frown knitted in his brow. "Shit. Look, I'm not gonna say anymore, okay? Find out for yourself." With that, he turned and walked back to the cottage, stopping at the front door. "There's a carnival tonight," he said, "wanna go?"

I didn't look at him. I just stared off at the last pieces of orange sky that were settling down behind the pine trees. "Yeah, sure," I muttered.

David turned to go inside then stopped. "Hey," he called over to me. I looked across the parking area at him. He had that smirk again. "Did you?" he asked.

"Did I what?" As if I didn't know what he was talking about.

"Did you do it to'er?"

The beet red blood rushed to my face. If he had been right in front of me, I would have dropped him.

"Come on I gotta know. Did you ball'er or not."

I didn't raise my voice. I just stared across the parking circle at my lifelong friend and simply said, "Fuck you, David."

"Oh, yeah, I forgot, you're in love," he retorted. Then he just had to take one more shot. "Don't forget, if you dropped your load in'er and knocked'er up, your kid might come out all fucked-up with a pointy head an' have to be thrown off the cliff." He had a sickeningly sweet sarcastic expression on his face as he quickly walked up the steps, disappeared inside, and slammed the door.

Yet, again, I found myself standing alone in front of the little white summer cottage at dusk.

Fuck you, I'd said to David, my best friend since birth. Fuck you and all your fucking bullshit stories. What was happening to me? In just two days, I was actually feeling what I could only describe as 'hatred' towards David. I was using all of his favorite words on him. Not just mine – his. And, they were coming easier to me.

Big Red nosed open the front door and trotted over to me. I reached down and stroked his head, as he rubbed up against my leg. Suddenly, something moved. Over among the trees. Both Big Red and I heard a twig snap at the same time. I squinted, trying to see into the darkness that had folded in around the cottage. Big Red growled a warning. Someone was standing just within the trees near the far side of the cottage, a dark, hunched figure. My eyes focused on the shadowy image, as it slowly turned away and shuffled quietly back into the woods and was gone. I stood there for a moment. Wondering who could have been watching from the woods. A cold shiver ran through me.

Somewhere I'd read, or heard someplace, that animals, like dogs and cats, have some sort of inner sixth sense and can actually feel the pain and suffering a human is going through. I'm not really sure about that. All I do know is Big Red always seemed to know when I was feeling bad and tried to do something about it. Usually, with a face-lick or an affectionate rub up against my leg. I never questioned it. I was just glad he was there. I dropped down and quietly wrapped my arms around Big Red's neck, just as I'd done when I was little and needed his comfort, as the fog began to drift in through the trees.

ELEVEN

THE CARNIVAL

The carnival wasn't at all like the ones back home. Our annual county fair was something that David and I had always looked forward to with great anticipation. We'd spend an entire year planning just how and where we would sneak onto the fairgrounds to beat the entrance fee. It never dawned on us that this ritual had been in place as far back as when our grandfathers were young; and, that the organizers of the fair wanted as many kids inside as possible - because kids meant parents and parents meant money. It was great fun. Everything from 4-H farm exhibits to homemade pie eating contests, greyhound dog races, all kinds of rides, an honest-to-goodness rodeo, and a fantastic midway with live sideshows.

One year, they even had "Dancing Cassandra and her Amazing Python." On that particular August day, David and I tried to sneak under the tent flap to see her show, but were caught red-handed and delivered over to the police tent for a stern lecture. We never told our parents about that little episode and, we never did get to see what Cassandra did with her amazing snake. The next day, her tent was no longer on the midway, courtesy of the matrons from the local historical society, half of whom went to high school with the Police Chief's father. However, the torrid stories that circulated from those fortunate enough to get in, before poor Cassandra was summarily run out of town, kept David's tongue wagging and my dreams active for several months.

David drove Petey and me up a dark dirt road toward a wide-open field, about five miles outside of town. All I could see, from the station wagon, was one Ferris wheel and a Tilt-A-Whirl at the end of two lines of cupie doll and sucker game tents that formed a sort of dimly lighted midway. David pulled off the road onto a bumpy field parking area that was already filled with all the battered pickup trucks and junkers from the barn dance the night before.

I was really in a rotten mood, ever since David confronted me with all the crazy stuff about Sandy. I'd already decided that I wasn't going to believe a word of it and, even if her old kinda-boyfriend showed up, I didn't care. It was her choice to be with me and no one else's. Also, there was no way Sandy could ever be related to either Petey or Ira Peak. All you had to do was look at her. She didn't have the slightest resemblance to either of them - or to anyone else around the town for that matter. That meant that her real father could not have been from around there. But, none of it mattered to me. I desperately wanted to be with her again... just like we were on top of the mountain that afternoon... *I'm just glad it was with me...*

David parked the station wagon in the dark, next to a row of backwoods jalopies. The three of us had been passing around one of Petey's rotgut bottles, since we left Big Red back at the cottage. I was sucking on it pretty good, trying to drop my anger down to a manageable level, before we got to the carnival.

"Hey, go easy on that," David warned, as I took another slug of the 150 proof whiskey. "We got the whole night ahead of us." I handed the bottle back to David. Just in time. I was about to buy another ticket to ride the roller coaster.

We got out of the station wagon and started making our way through the unlighted tangle of haphazardly parked cars, toward the carnival area. As we squeezed between two vintage pickup trucks, I heard something in the shadows to my right and stopped. It looked like a fight. I stepped over the bumpers of two old cars to get a better look. About five or six local guys had another man surrounded and were beating the crap out of him. They each took a turn smashing him in the face or kicking him anywhere they could make contact. His white tee-shirt was soaked with the blood that was streaming from his nose and mouth.

"Jesus," I whispered to myself; then jumped when David's hand grabbed me on the shoulder from behind.

"Come on," he said in a hush, just as one of the bigger guys kicked the poor bastard right square in the nuts. The man heaved his guts up right there and dropped to his knees, groaning pathetically. The local mouth-breathers laughed and poured beer and rotgut over their fresh kill... *the frog!...the frog!...*

David jerked me back as the part of me that doesn't think, when I see an injustice like that taking place, was about ready to leap into the circle of crazies to rescue the victim in distress. "Leave'im alone," David rasped, "s'none of our business."

"But, God... We gotta help. They're gonna kill'im!"

"He's just a fuckin' Indian. Come on."

We headed out of the parking area and passed a battered old Ford with someone seated in it on the passenger side. It was Cyrus Peak the cripple, hunched over, drinking from a pint bottle of whiskey in the dark. He looked up at me with his one disfigured eye. I really didn't react, although I sort of nodded a little, and then hurried after David and Petey who were heading for the midway.

The carnival was even sleazier than it had looked from the distance. The sucker game tents were all dark and greasy and the cupie doll prizes looked as if no one had ever won anything beyond the level of plastic whirligig-birds-on-a-stick. I couldn't tell the carny people from the small crowd of locals who were cheerlessly dragging themselves up and down the short, depressing midway with their mouths hanging open.

The picture of the Indian being massacred was still in my head. "Man, they were really trying to kill that guy," I said to David, as we walked along.

"S'none of our business."

"It was six against one," I protested.

We stopped at a lead bottle game. David handed the carny guy a dollar and took the three dirt-caked, weighted baseballs from him. "He's an Indian," David said and let go with a baseball that missed the stack of lead bottles completely.

"So what?" I said.

David reached back and let the second ball go, smashing the stack of lead bottles right on target. Only three out of the six fell off the platform. "That's what they do to Indians up here."

"Why?"

David gave the third ball a halfhearted toss and we turned back up the midway. "How should I know?" David said. He was getting increasingly annoyed with my persistence. "They're supposed to stay in the woods that's all I know." I glanced over at Petey, who was meandering along picking at his hair and not paying much attention to anything in particular, let alone the plight of the American Indian.

I looked around for Sandy, but didn't see her. David and I played a few of the sucker games, without winning much of anything. I won a goldfish in a plastic bag for landing a quarter in a dish. I wasn't about to carry it around, so I just walked away and left the carny guy holding the bag. I figured anyone who had an eagle tattooed across his forehead needed a goldfish more than I did.

We passed around Petey's bottle a couple of times and were about ready to buy tickets for the Tilt-A-Whirl, when David spotted something on up the midway and shouted out, "Hey, there's a strip show."

I wasn't really all that interested, but headed for the strip show tent with David and Petey anyway. I still hadn't been able to spot Sandy anywhere and was beginning to think she wasn't going to show up. The strip show tent reminded me of "Dancing Cassandra and her Amazing Python" back at our county fair. An old, seedy barker stepped up onto a wooden platform in front of a large painting of "Lady Velma" spread out over a paint-chipped canvas, strung up between two poles. She didn't have a python, but the painting made her out to have the biggest tits in the world.

There were already several slovenly local kindred

gaping blankly up at the voluminous work of art. The tired, old barker listlessly started his spiel through a scratchy bullhorn, as we strolled up. "It ain't nothin' like you ever seed before," the barker droned. "The Lady Velma will bring out the animal in you. Her hot-dance-from-hell will heat you up like you ain't never been heated up before. Jus' five lousy dollars will get you inside the sexiest X-rated show of the century." I could just imagine the reactions of the ladies from the historical society if they could get a load of this.

David was already reaching into his pocket for his wallet and edging up toward the front. He motioned to Petey and me to come with him. From the expression on his face, I could see that David was already sold and nothing was going to stop him this time. I wondered if he'd been harboring bad feelings, ever since we got caught trying to sneak into Cassandra's tent. I mean, that was such a long time ago. But, with David, anything was possible.

"You guys comin' with me? I'm goin' in," David said, his eyes bright with anticipation.

The barker heard David and figured he had a live one. "How'bout you boys?" he rasped through his bullhorn. "Remember, foist ones inside get right up close to all the action."

David had his wallet out. "You comin' or not?" he challenged me.

"Nah, I'm supposed to meet Sandy...and..." Petey shot me a look that had 'warning' written all over it. But, I still didn't care.

"Come on, don't be a jerk-off, I'll buy." Before I could stop him, David was at the ticket booth buying three tickets to see Lady Velma and her 'hot-dance-from-hell.'

Inside the grimy, dank tent, that smelled like my grandmother's old root cellar back home, a string of bare bulbs were strung around a narrow wooden stage, about five feet off the dirt floor. A faded red velvet curtain, with fold marks crisscrossing it, stretched across a pipe frame at the rear; where I assumed Lady Velma was waiting out of sight to make her grand entrance.

David quickly staked out his position right up front next to the stage, with Petey and me on either side of him. I looked around as twenty, or so, gaunt locals filed in behind us, cradling their hooch bottles that they started passing around amongst themselves. Petey did the same with David and me. David took a big gulp to fortify himself, then passed me the bottle with a big grin. I slugged down some of the hot swill and passed it back to Petey. My head was starting to swim. Then, from an old wooden, cloth-covered speaker hanging above the pipe frame, the scratchy sounds of thumping exotic music filled the tent.

"Here she comes," David announced to me, his eyes glittering with anticipation.

The barker came in through the tent flap entrance and pulled a rope at the side of the pipe frame that jerked the red velvet curtain open. And, there she was in all her aging beauty.

"Laaaaaady...Veeeeeelllma," the barker blurted through his bullhorn. "Give'er a hand."

David clapped enthusiastically. "Shit. Look at those fuckin' tits," he whispered excitedly in my ear.

They were big alright. Huge. Enormous. Just like the ones in David's stash of big boob magazines. I just stood there staring at the sagging, crusty woman with the powder-white makeup and dyed black hair that hung in oily twirls down around the wrinkled, sad old face of someone who'd died inside a long time ago. She stared blankly, through heavily made-up eyes, out at the men looking impassively up at her and teased them with the see-through veil that she held up around most of her dumpy body. I wondered if Cassandra had looked like Lady Velma and decided that, maybe, the matrons had been right to run her out of town after all.

The music thumped into a dance rhythm and Lady Velma vamped forward, absently twirling her veil around as she emitted little high-pitched squeals. She neared the front of the stage and dropped the veil to reveal her frayed, red sequined bra and G-string stripper costume. Some of which had disappeared into the fat creases around her middle. She also had, what appeared to be, a fair number of old bruises. Here, there, and pretty much everywhere. Not a fact that would have made any significant difference to David.

I guess I must have been really staring at her intensely because when she gave me a big wink, I jumped inside. David laughed out loud. The beets raced to my face and I wished we were standing in the back of the tent, instead of right up front. Actually, I wished I wasn't even inside the tent at all.

Lady Velma slid down the pipe frame onto the stage and gave it a few halfhearted humps, then got back up and started 'tempting' her audience by toying with the clasps on her sequined bra and G-string. David elbowed me excitedly. Lady Velma popped her bra hook in back, but deftly stopped it from falling, by placing her costumed-jeweled hand against her bountiful bosom. She acted surprised and squealed, "Ooo..." Then, she reached under her bra and began to fondle one of her breasts.

"Whoa!" David breathed out, completely enthralled.

The exotic music built to a thumping crescendo and the sequined bra hit the floor of the stage. Lady Velma held both of her hands spread over her breasts and vamped forward, right over our heads. The stage was just high enough to nearly reach up under our chins, so we were almost looking straight up. The music thumped and bumped. Suddenly, Lady Velma let the dam burst and the mammoth set of stretch-marked, blue-veined mammaries flopped out and down, landing with a slap on Lady Velma's rubbery stomach.

David gazed up. Mouth hanging open. Speechless. His eyes transfixed on the two colossal bags of flesh, as the Lady Velma bent over and shook her massive udders right over him. Something must have struck her funny bone, because a big, gap-toothed grin spread across her white-powdered, sagging face, as she looked right down into David's wide eyes. The music slowed. Lady Velma got down on her knees right in front of us and let her monstrous breasts sway back and fourth to the rhythm. I glanced back at the locals. Some of them were grinning toothless grins. The others just stood there with their usual, faraway, mouth-breather expressions. I looked back. Lady Velma stood up and started strutting and squealing around the narrow stage, toying with the clasps on her red-sequined G-string.

"Here it comes," David whispered excitedly to Petey and me.

With a flip-turn and her back to her audience, Lady

Velma flicked her wrist with practiced precision and the sparkling G-string flew into the air and disappeared into the darkness behind the red velvet curtain. The music thumped slowly. Lady Velma's large, white, dimpled bare rear end floated and rippled from side to side. I could hear David's breath coming in short pants. I looked at Petey. His expression hadn't changed at all. He just watched with his beady eyes glued to Lady Velma's big butt. At least, he wasn't picking at his scalp.

David's eyes danced with delight. Lady Velma turned to face us. Did she ever. All of her, except the part between her bulging thighs that she had hidden under her strategically placed hand. "Come-on-come-on," David gritted to himself.

Lady Velma must have heard David's urgent plea, because she moved forward, tippy-step-by-tippy-step, until she stood directly overhead, straddling David's upturned face at the edge of the stage. She grinned down at him. Taunting him. David stood there, bug-eyed. She swayed to-and-fro, her hand clamped between her legs. The music thumped a cue. Her fingers snapped apart. David's eyes widened. So did mine. Then, ever-so-slowly, Lady Velma pulled her costume jeweled hand away and ran it up over her protruding belly. Her body arched backwards on down into a full backbend, that ended up with the top of her head touching the stage and her fully exposed 'special attraction' just inches from David's astonished face.

"Holy shit!" David uttered incredulously, as he stared right into the unbelievable sight before him.

Suddenly, Lady Velma dropped to the stage and, in one fluid motion, rolled to a standup position, completely wrapped in the veil she'd begun her 'hot- dance-from-hell' with. In a flash, she disappeared behind the threadbare red velvet curtain that the barker was already jerking closed from just inside the tent flap entrance. The music stopped.

David's mouth was still hanging open. "Man," he uttered. "Did you see that big ugly snapper?" Then, he started laughing out loud. "God, I'm never gonna eat another clam as long as I live." He turned to Petey. "Gimme a drink before I throw up." Petey took the bottle out from under his shirt and handed it to David.

The sound of the barker's voice grating through his bullhorn startled me. "Awright, listen up. For just two dollars more, you don't have to wait outside for the next show. All you gotta do is pony up a measly two bucks an' you get to see somethin' the next group won't. You get to see the Lady Velma do her very own X-rated, world famous, disappearing trick. Yes-yes, for only two pieces of worthless government paper, you get to see Lady Velma..." He took a roll of quarters out of his pocket and placed it on the stage and droned on, "...make this stack of quarters disappear from this here bottle." He placed a full, capped soda bottle beside the roll of quarters and started stacking the coins on top of it. "That's right folks. I mean, you ain't seen nothin' 'til you seen Lady Velma suck this here stack of quarters right up into her little hole-of-hell."

Lady Velma was one 'hell' of a lady alright. I saw David reaching into his pocket for his wallet. "Hey, I'll see you guys later," I said.

"Whudda-you-mean?" David said, as he hurriedly took some money out of his wallet. "You're not gonna miss this for crissakes?"

"Yeah, I'll meet you by the Ferris wheel in half an hour."

David's expression dimmed and his eyes hardened. "Hey, have it your way. I mean, what's Lady Velma got that you haven't already seen with Sandy, right?" At that moment, it was a good thing that the old barker stepped between us to collect David's money. I turned away, without saying anything more, and walked outside.

I stood out in front of Lady Velma's tent for a moment and wondered what the hell was eating David so much. It was like he wasn't the same person I'd grown up with for fifteen years. I mean, I was on a trip with my best friend. A trip that we had planned ever since David got his license. We'd spent over six months cajoling David's parents - his mother really - that we could handle the trip alone. In fact, I had to assure her that I would never let David out of my sight. I wondered how she'd react at seeing her son staring into Lady Velma's 'hole-of-hell.' I tried to imagine her explaining it to the good Reverend Stevens. Although, David had informed me that he'd heard that both the good Reverend and his wife had been dipping into his flock for quite some time.

I wandered along the midway for awhile. There was a skee-ball game. I played and won enough orange tickets for a plastic whirligig-bird-on-a-stick. I accepted my prize. At least, I wouldn't have to feed it. I ate a greasy hot dog and washed it down with something resembling yellow sugar water and still no Sandy anywhere in sight.

...What the hell was going on? Why was David being such a fucking asshole? It couldn't be about just going out with Sandy. I mean, David and I had been best friends forever. We'd done everything together. We dug a hole almost to China at the beach. We'd gone skinny-dipping every summer at the river. David had even shown me what to do behind the bush that day. Our secret club had been our secret and no one else's. When David got caught with the stink bomb at camp, I told the camp director that it was my idea too. It wasn't my fault that he didn't believe me. I was right behind David when we tried to sneak in to see "Dancing Cassandra and her Amazing Python." And, it was David who showed me how to pop eggs out of a chicken's butt so we could press our fingerprints into the wet shell before it dried. When he told me how he'd boffed both Mary and Margaret at the same time, I just laughed it off and made believe it was great news. Even though I knew it couldn't be true. I even went so far as to tell the football coach that I thought David would make a good quarterback. So what the hell was going on?

Maybe, it was me. Maybe I was the one to blame for why David was being such a shithead. But, that didn't make any sense. I'd even gone on the skunk run and I'd watched him catch 'the bird' with the cattail and we'd laughed together until we were sick to our stomachs from Petey's rotgut. And I was right there, if he'd needed me, when Ira Peak pulled the station wagon out of the creek. In fact, come to think of it, I was always there to defend David. I had always been there. No matter what. God, when Patricia saw me sitting with David's little gum-popper friend, I never let on that I had a funny feeling about how I'd ended up in the passion pit in the first place.

The thought of Patricia, and how she would have liked our county fair, made me sad. I'd had it in the back of my mind to just pull it together and call her, when we got back home, to ask her if she'd go out with me again. Maybe, I could have won her a big Panda or taken her on the Ferris wheel and had a chance to explain to her that I wasn't really with that other girl. And, that I'd waited outside the Orpheum Theater for her and thought she wasn't coming, because her father hadn't given her permission. I'm sure she'd have understood. But, since spending the afternoon up on the mountain, everything had changed. I wasn't the same anymore and I knew that I would probably never have a chance to explain to Patricia how I really felt about her... *I'm just glad it was with me...*

The hot dog sank right to the bottom of my stomach and mixed in with all of Petey's rotgut I'd had to drink on the way to the carnival. I walked along the small midway, past the dreary sucker game tents. Small groups of hollow-eyed natives watched their hollow-eyed cousins, or brothers, or mother-fathers, lose their money throwing darts at deflated balloons, or trying to knock over dirty, fur-rimmed doll targets with old black-taped baseballs. There was a strange smell in the air. Almost like the dead dog David and Big Red and I found in the woods near our secret club.

I was feeling pretty sorry for myself and began thinking about my mother and what she'd think if she knew how her only son had spent the afternoon on the mountain. It's not that my mother was a prude or anything. In fact, we got along quite well and, compared to what David had to go through with his, mine was pretty open to discussing sex and things. But, that wasn't the point. The point was that David and I were supposed to be 'having a hell of a time' - as he kept telling me we would ever since he'd first hatched his plan to take the trip. It was a 'hell' of a time alright. And, God. I thought of God. He knew what I'd done. And, I was quite certain that He'd never let me forget it. That's how strong an influence God had where we lived. Not that I was all that religious, or even that my parents were, but I always had this underlying fear of God. Maybe, it had to do with my heritage, which my grandfather said went all the way back to Salem and the witches and the witch trials. My guilt, for what I'd done, began to override my senses and get the better of me. I hardly knew Sandy. And yet, I had...I had... What if she got pregnant? What would I do then? I was only fifteen. I wasn't even out of high school.

Fear grabbed my brain and my mind raced. She would never be able to find me after David and I left. She even told me that she had only been to the next town only once in her life. Petey had never even seen a train. Maybe, she had thrown a baby off the cliff. But, that wasn't true. That was just one of David's wild stories. I actually tried to fantasize that none of it had happened and that there was no Sandy and no Petey and that it was just my friend David and me having... one hell of a time.

No. It wouldn't be right. It would be my fault, if she had a baby. It would be my responsibility... "Three rings for a buck"...It would be my responsibility. I would have to take care of... "Three rings for a buck"...I wouldn't let them throw my baby off the cliff. I'd find a way to take care of it... "Three rings for a buck"...

"What?"

A hollow-eyed carny guy hawked a huge yellow loogie out in front of me, from inside a ringtoss tent, and asked me if I wanted to play. "Three rings for a buck." I politely declined his gracious offer and moved on - wishing we'd never come to this godforsaken place.

I thought of David. This wasn't the way it was supposed to be. Not at all. David had promised that we were going to have fun. It was our first time away from home without any supervision and it was all turning out wrong. I mean, we had talked about how we were going to get laid, and David had said over and over again that, "these hicky girls really put out." But, I'd never thought I would actually 'do it' with anyone.

David had me very confused. Ever since I could remember, David had always been a little crazy and very intense, but that's why I liked him. That's why I'd been his friend for so long. He made me laugh and, because I was just naturally kind of shy, he made me think about things I probably wouldn't even have thought of. At least, not in the different ways he thought of things...

Ira Peak...Ira Peak... Shit! Ira Peak was standing with his two drinking buddies next to the beer tent. I quickly glanced around to see if Sandy was nearby. No sight of her anywhere. I was pretty sure Ira hadn't seen me. I turned around and started walking back along the midway toward Lady Velma's strip show. As I walked hurriedly past a narrow dark passageway between two sideshow tents, someone reached out and grabbed me by my throat. I was jerked back into the shadows and shoved down hard onto my knees in the semidarkness. I looked up into the gaunt, grinning faces of the two men standing over me. Ira Peak's friends.

"What...what do you want?" I stammered, suddenly wrapped in fear.

"Giddup," one of them growled with a sadistic, twisted grin. "Someone wants'ta talk to-ya."

I got up slowly... thinking... if I ducked between the two mouth-breathers and ran for it, I could make it back to Lady Velma's tent. David would be there to help me. We had a bond and... we had a bond...and...

I made a dive for the midway. One of them hooked my ankle with his foot. I hit the ground hard. Face first. I felt myself being dragged, belly-down, by my feet, along the narrow passageway toward the rear of the tents. I reached out and grabbed ahold of a wooden tent stake and held on. I saw someone out there on the midway. I saw Sandy. She was standing out there with Mildred. Ira's two friends jerked and pulled at my legs. "Sandy!" I shouted as loud as I could, just as a gypsy organ-grinder with a monkey on a leash passed in front of her, cranking out a loud tune. Sandy turned and looked behind her, but not between the tents toward me. She moved away and disappeared in the direction of the Ferris wheel.

One of the men kicked at my hands, trying to get me to let go of the tent stake. The other one kicked me hard right over my eye. I saw stars and felt my hands weaken and lose their grip. I saw the skinny organ-grinder's monkey curiously looking in my direction from the midway. He tipped his little jester hat and offered his tin collection cup, just as they dragged me by my ankles around the back corner of a tent, through some wet garbage and into the middle of a small clearing. There, they let go. My feet hit the ground toes first. It was very dark, except for the dim glow from the midway. I was breathing hard right into the dirt. My heart was pounding in my ears... *the frog!...the frog!...*

I tried to focus my eyes in the darkness. Something warm and wet was running down my face. Blood! My head had been cut open from the kick. I heard someone's shoes shuffling toward me in the darkness and stop just inches from my face. I didn't dare move.

"Think you kin come up he'ah an' jes' diddle any woman you wants, don't'cha city-boy?"

I looked up. A crease of light shined in from between the tents and slashed across Ira Peak's hollow black eyes, as he stared down at me. I didn't get a chance to speak. Ira reached down and yanked me up onto my feet by my hair and jerked my face right into his. I could smell the thick stench of rotgut and rotten teeth on his breath, as he hissed, "Think you kin hump anythin' you wants." Then, with his free hand, he started slapping my face with little stinging slaps.

"Please...please, don't..." My voice was a hoarse whisper.

"Think you better'n us. Think we-ah all dumb an' stupid."

"No...I..."

Ira tightened his grip on my hair and reached into his pocket with his other hand. He jammed my head down so my chin hit my chest. I could see the glint of the Buck knife he held in his hand. Slowly, he ran the knife point up and down the zipper of my fly. Then, Ira turned to his friends. "Go git that Sandy girl an' t'other city-boy. I want'em t'see this," he said, grinning wide. They took off as ordered.

I was alone in the darkness with Ira. He looked back at me, his black eyes dancing in the slash of light that crossed his face. "City-boy think he got a big'ah stick than

I do." He jabbed the knife point up into my crotch, jarring me onto my tiptoes. I could feel the sharp point of the blade stabbing through my jeans into my...

"Well, I ain't gonna have'ta worry no more 'bout where you puts that big pig-stick-ah of yo'ahs."

I tried to cry out, but couldn't... *the frog!...the frog!...* My head hammered inside. This couldn't be happening to me. Not me. I never hurt anyone... *Patricia...* But, that wasn't my fault. It was... It was... I didn't kill the frog. I didn't kill the frog. It was... It was... I never made the sacrifice... But, I never lied to David. Not once. I always told him everything... except... except for...

"No, Ira," someone screamed from behind me. "Don't do it. Stop!" Sandy's voice. It was Sandy screaming at Ira.

Ira let go of my hair. His long thin arm whipped back like a snake and let go with a backhand that cracked across the side of Sandy's head so hard it sent her flying back into one of the tents. I wanted to run, but I couldn't feel my legs. They were frozen with fear and wouldn't work. I felt like I was going to collapse. Sandy scrambled to her feet and came at Ira again. But the friend of Ira's, who went after her, reached out, grabbed her by the wrist, swung her away and around in a wide circle. Faster and faster, until she fell over her feet and was cartwheeled up into the air and slammed down hard onto the ground.

Ira still had the knife pointed a few inches from my fly. He looked at Sandy sprawled in a heap, then back at me. "Shit," he hissed and suddenly banged his forehead right into my lips. I could taste my blood in my mouth and felt it running down my chin. Before I could react, his foot flew up at me - in slow motion. A bolt of white lightning flashed and split my body from between my legs up into my skull, exploding into a starburst of colors that filled my brain and burned out my sight with such ungodly pain that it sent me down onto the ground convulsing in agony. "I...I can't breathe," I rasped. Everything around me was going in reverse. I couldn't focus and started to black out.

"Oh, God! Noooo!" Sandy's scream echoed from someplace far away. "You fuckin' bastard," she shouted at Ira. I felt someone's body over mine. Someone's arms around me... soft arms... *Patricia?...* No... *Mother?...* No... *I'm just glad it was with me...*

“He's all yo’ahs now," Ira's voice chortled from the distance, "what's left of'im. Don't think he gonna be takin' you nowhe’ahs now girl. Ain't no one gonna take a pig like you nowhe’ah, no-how. You stuck he’ah forev’ah, girl. An' don't you go thinkin' no different or I'll run you down an' shoot you like a common field rabbit."

The excruciating pain was propelling everything from my stomach up into my throat. I could see shadows moving around me. A black-and-white form came around the tent and stopped in the slash of light. David? David had come to help me. Another dark form came up behind him... and, another... Petey Peak... with...with Ira's other friend... My sight flickered in and out. Ira walked past Petey... reached out... pinched and twisted Petey's nipple through his shirt and made a sucking noise. "Where you goin' queer-boy? Huh? You with them? You givin' them city-boys some'a yo’ah fun?” Three of the dark forms walked away and disappeared between the tents laughing. David's shadow came closer. "Jesus... what happened?"

The soft arms held my head. "What the hell's it look like?" I heard Sandy spit out at David.

David's shadow bent over me. "You okay, Billy?" His voice was distant and sounded very shaky.

"No, he's not. He's beat up real bad. Help me get'im up," I heard Sandy shout back at David. Then, she added angrily, "Why weren't you with'im?"

"I...I was just..." David's voice said weakly. I felt his and Sandy's arms pulling me up onto my feet. But, my legs didn't feel like they were a part of me. They started to walk me back toward the light between the tents. I tripped. "Come on, Billy," David said, hanging onto my arm.

As David and Sandy helped me back toward the midway, it felt like my whole body was swimming. I saw the tent stake I'd tried to hang onto. Someone was silhouetted at the entrance between the tents. Someone small... Mildred... with her arms clamped tightly over her caved-in chest. We stopped at the edge of the midway. Everything inside me suddenly erupted and let go through my nose and mouth. "Oh, no!" David exclaimed from somewhere outside my haze. He recoiled and let go of me. I hunched over and yielded to all of the burning vomit that flowed freely up and out of me.

"Hold'im up," Sandy shouted at David, as she tried to keep me from falling.

David grabbed my free arm. "What's the matter with him?" I heard him nervously ask.

"He's hurt, you stupid jerk."

The two of them held me until I'd gotten everything out of me and my head started to clear. "Hey, Billy?" David asked tentatively, still holding me by my arm, "You'll be okay...huh?...Right?..."

Why was David sounding so helpless and wussy? Just like he'd sounded when Big Red was accidentally peppered with birdshot by a pheasant hunter when he was almost ten and I was eight. I couldn't answer him. I was too weak. Besides, there were a bunch of black-and-white, open-mouthed shadows lurking around us. Gazing at me.

"We gotta get'im back to your place," Sandy said to David.

As they started to ease me up the midway, I spotted something lying on the ground in front of me. My whirligig-bird-on-a-stick prize. I broke free of Sandy and David and dropped to my knees and picked up my whirligig-bird.

"Come on, Billy," David urged.

"No," I blurted out and slowly started waving the whirligig-bird out in front of me from my kneeling position. "See," I muttered, "I didn't kill the bird. It's still alive, see. I didn't kill it."

David and Sandy lifted me back up onto my feet and, with Petey Peak who had been following along, they slowly led me past the sucker game tents toward the dark field where the station wagon was parked. I held onto my whirligig-bird out in front of me, as I stumbled along between them. The last tent, at the end of the midway, was higher than the rest and had a bright floodlight shining on the side of it. As I staggered forward into the field, supported between David and Sandy, I looked back at the tent and thought I saw the dark silhouetted image of the 'demon dog' splayed up over it.

We had just started back through the tangle of tightly parked cars and pickup trucks, when I suddenly broke free of Sandy and David and hurriedly began to scramble between the junkers. "Hey, Billy," David shouted and ran after me. "Where're you goin?"

"I gotta find'im," I yelled out. "I gotta help'im." The sudden sharp pain in my shin, smashing into a protruding steel bumper, sent me spinning off against a truck fender and down hard on my seat. Still holding tightly to my whirligig-bird.

David came leaping over the bumper. "What the hell're you doing?"

I tried to focus on David's dark shadow standing over me in the semidarkness. I couldn't make out his face. Why didn't he understand? "We gotta help'im," I said.

"Help who?"

"The Indian. We gotta help the Indian before they kill him."

"Oh, shit," David's shadow blurted out, then reached down and hauled me to my feet... *the frog!...the frog!...*

"Gimme the bottle," I demanded through my swollen lips, as Sandy and David helped me onto the back seat of the station wagon. I couldn't help groaning. The monstrous ache between my legs was throbbing like hell.

"Give'im the bottle," David ordered Petey, in his drill sergeant voice. Too little, too late, I thought to myself. More interested in watching Lady Velma suck up quarters with her hell-hole than helping his best friend.

Petey handed me a nearly full bottle of rotgut through the opened window. I took a long swig and clutched the bottle so no one could take it away. The rancid stuff didn't burn my throat, which I figured was probably covered with scar tissue from throwing up so much. Just like Petey's.

Sandy leaned in. "You gonna be alright, Billy?" she

asked with real concern in her voice. I mumbled something and took another slug of rotgut. She kissed me lightly on my forehead, then leaned back out and spoke to David. "Me an' Mildred'll follow you over to your place."

"Yeah-okay," David said, still sounding like a weak chickenshit.

I watched Sandy take Mildred by the hand and lead her off between the parked cars into the darkness. David and Petey got into the front of the station wagon and we drove away from the carnival. I looked back to see if the 'demon dog' was still silhouetted in the light shining on the tent. It wasn't. The rotgut was doing its job, easing the pain between my legs, but my head was beginning to fog up. "Gimme back my yellow pail," I think I said.

"What?" David replied, with more than a little surprise in his voice.

"Never mind," I muttered and rested my head back on the seat and closed my eyes.

TWELVE

BIG RED

...The black-and-white fiend was enveloped in a hazy light under a shroud of darkness. He was alone this time. No other freaks gathered around him. Actually, he was smiling down at me, which meant I must have been looking up at him. He murmured something, but I couldn't quite catch what he'd said...

"...Billy...Billy...Billy..." Sandy... Sandy was looking down at me. "You were sleepin'," she said softly. I glanced around. I shouldn't have moved my head. My brain thumped so hard against the inside of my skull that I had to close my eyes for a moment. When I opened them again, I realized that I was stretched out on the couch in the cottage with my head in Sandy's lap. Big Red was asleep on the braided rug on the other side of the coffee table.

"Where's David?" I asked. My lips felt like they were twice the size as they should be.

"He gave Mildred an' Petey a ride home."

Through the haze, I spotted the half full bottle of rotgut whiskey on the coffee table and reached for it. As I slowly sat up, my whole body felt like it had been hit by a train.

"Don't drink no more," Sandy said, "you're pretty

drunk already."

I tipped the bottle back and let the crystal clear liquid run down my cauterized gullet. The putrid stuff hit me right between the eyes. I looked at Sandy seated at the other end of the couch. There were two of her looking back at me. Both of them had a very sad look on their faces. I took another drink to snap my vision back. It seemed to work.

"Billy," Sandy said.

"Mmmmm..." I managed to reply.

"You hurt huh."

"Mmmmm..." I grunted. I hurt like hell. I gulped some more 150 proof to help keep the pain at bay.

"I'm real sorry, Billy."

I didn't say anything. The whiskey was really working on me.

"Billy?"

"Mmmmm?"

She waited and looked away from me before she continued, "Do...do you feel the same?"

I still couldn't answer her.

"Billy?" she asked again.

"What?" was all I could muster.

Sandy looked away from me again for a long moment. When she looked back, I could see the pained expression in her eyes. "Do you still feel the same?" she asked.

"About what?" I mumbled through my split lips.

Sandy stared right into my eyes. I squinted and tried to focus on her face, through the long, murky tunnel I was in. The only thing I could make out was that she seemed to be searching for something... wanting me to say something to her.

"About us," she said, almost as if she were truly afraid to say it.

I sat there, feeling very shaky. I upended the bottle of rotgut and finished it off in two big gulps.

"Please tell me, Billy," I heard her say at the other end of the long tunnel. "If you don't...I...I wish you'd just tell me."

What was she talking about? What did she want me to tell her? I shook my head, trying to clear it, trying hard to pull the words through my brain. Then, I suddenly blurted out, "Do-you-have-a-kid?"

I couldn't see Sandy. She was so far away...way at the very end of the endless tunnel. But, I surely felt the sudden and extreme change of emotion that shot through her.

"What?" Sandy uttered in shocked disbelief.

I rounded up my scramble of words and tried to put them together more cohesively. "Do-you... Did-you... have-a-child?"

I squinted hard and could just make out the confusion on Sandy's face. "No," she said in a near whisper, "I've never even been..." Then, her voice became harsh and distant. "Who...who told you that?" she insisted.

"Doesn't matter," I mumbled. I looked away and tried to suck the last drop out of the rotgut bottle. It was dry. I let it slip out of my hand onto the floor. The hazy fog was settling into my head again. I looked at Sandy and could see the glint of moisture gathering in her eyes. She started to stand up. She was leaving. *...She was going to run out of the Orpheum Theater and I'd never see her again...* I lurched across the couch and jerked her back down beside me.

"I'm sorry," I managed to say. I wasn't going to let her get away again. Not again.

Her words came spilling out of her, "I...I thought you wanted me to be yours and..." She started to cry. "Billy, I never met anyone like you before now. You're so different. You're everythin' I been dreamin' about since I was little. I mean... maybe... maybe, I could go with you. We could be together. Maybe we could get a boat and I could teach you an'... an' someday, we could have a house like this one an'... an'... I'm real good on the boats, Billy... Billy?..."

I squinted and desperately tried to focus. Something was wrong. She didn't look the same... the same as...

"Oh, God, Billy! Say you love me," she pleaded tearfully. "Please don't spoil it. Say we'll be together always."

...But, if you're not Patricia...Who are you?...

"Billy... Billy, you just gotta say you love me. I can't stay here no longer. I'll die if I don't get outta here. Please, Billy, please take me with you."

From far away, David's voice jumped in *...She's just lookin' for someone to get'er out of here, that's all. Anyone...* Then Ira rasped *...Ain't no one gonna take a pig like you nowhe'ah, no-how. You stuck he-ah forev'ah, girl...*

"I...I..." I couldn't see her face. Everything was getting blurred and dark. Someone's arms were around me.

"Oh, Billy... Billy, I love you. You're everythin' I ever hoped for all my life."

Someone kissed me on my cheek... my lips... I pulled back and tried hard to concentrate, but all I could see was a shadow next to me.

"Billy? What is it?"

"Huh?"

"You...you want me, don't you? You love me, too, don't you? Billy...you want me to go with you. I mean, when you go back home. You want me to go back home. You want me to go back with you, don't you?"

The shadow in front of me was getting darker and harder to see.

"Billy, please answer me. You're scaring me. You meant all those things you said, didn't you? I...I want us to live together an' be married... Billy?"

...You're not...You're not...Patricia...

"Billy...I want to have a baby with you."

...I'm just glad it was with me...

"Please, Billy. You gotta take me away from here. You just gotta take me with you."

"You... you're the one from... from up on... the mountain..."

"Yes, Billy, yes!"

The shadowed figure next to me started to fumble frantically with the front of herself... her blouse... taking it off... "Billy, take me. Now. Please take me, now."

I stood up into the darkness that was rapidly closing in around me. "I...I...want..." I muttered, trying in vain to pull a thought out of the fog.

"Yes. Oh, God, Billy, I want you too. It's gonna be so wonderful. I promise it will."

"...You're not..." The darkness filled in the light... "You're not... Patricia." I drifted slowly downward. Falling. A distant sound of something breaking all around me. No feeling. Then, nothing... except... except for the echo of voices in the darkness...

"Well, look what we have here. How're you gonna get outta here, now, huh?" David said sarcastically. "He never would've taken you, ya-know. Hey, I know Billy like the back of my hand. We've been blood-brothers-by-the-knife since we were little kids. We even have a bond and a sacrifice. He wouldn't've taken you with'im, because he hasn't got the guts. He's not like you an' me. We're different. Ya-know what I mean? Huh? You picked the wrong guy. You really wanna get outta here? I'll take you outta here. I'll take you back with me."

"I...please...I..."

"Hey, the way I see it, you got only two choices. You get to stay here with ol' Ira the rest of your life. Or, you choose me. Come on. Come on."

...Come on, Patricia... Patricia was standing barefoot in the brook, her white gossamer dress flowing easily in the summer breeze. Framed in a dense patch of white birch trees, she was smiling right at me. Her face was peaceful and radiant. But, where was I? I was standing just a few feet away on the edge of the rippling stream. But, I couldn't see me there, even though Patricia was looking at me. She smiled. I stepped forward, closer to the edge of the water. *...Come on, Patricia...* a voice called. But, it wasn't my voice. I tried to step into the water, but I couldn't move. Something was stopping me. *...Come on, Patricia...* "I'll take you out of here. I'll take you back with me." Again, I tried to step into the stream, but I was bound where I was. A dark figure stepped silently out of the patch of birch trees behind Patricia. *...Come on, Patricia...* She smiled at me. I couldn't make out the features of the

figure behind her. There wasn't any color... black-and-white. The black-and-white demon *...Come with me, Patricia...* She smiled once more, letting the breeze carry her gossamer dress away from her nude body... *"I'm just glad it was with me..."* she said in a lilting voice, then turned and walked lightly out of the running water, back toward the dark figure and accepted the hand that was extended to her...They walked away into the patch of birch trees and were gone...

...Big Red ran out of the surrounding woods and splashed through the stream up to me, as I stood, holding my bicycle, looking across the way at the patch of white birch trees. "Come on, Big Red. We gotta find David before it gets dark." I peddled my bike over the bumpy back farm road that wound down through the cow pastures toward the woods. Big Red sensed my anxiousness because he stopped and sniffed at every spot where he thought he'd picked up David's scent.

David's mother had called me a half-hour earlier telling me that David was late getting home and asked if I knew where he was; since she'd assumed he was with me. I told her I hadn't seen him since we'd walked home from school. She'd sounded very upset and asked me if I would please help find him. I said that I would, without telling her I knew exactly where he was. David would be hiding in the only place he'd go to whenever he'd run away from home, which wasn't often. But it did happen occasionally after he and his mother had really gotten into it. It was also a place he couldn't be found, except by me and Big Red.

I turned off the road onto the narrow path our bikes had flattened through the woods. Big Red jumped on ahead, knowing instinctively where I was headed. David's bike was leaning up against our secret clubhouse, just like I knew it would be. The door was closed. I left Big Red outside in the gathering dusk, to guard against anyone - or any 'thing' from sneaking up on us, and went inside.

David was seated at the old wooden table with his head buried in his arms. The candle in the middle of the table was lit. David hadn't looked up when I came in and closed the door behind me, although he knew it was me because I'd spoken to Big Red outside. David and I were the only ones who knew about our secret club. Not even our parents knew, because of the bond we had between us.

I sat down at the table. "What's the matter?" I asked. David didn't move. "Geez, your mother's really worried. She was cryin' when she called me."

"Fuck my mother," David said, his voice muffled in his arms.

I wasn't too surprised at his saying that about his mother, although I'd never even thought of saying it about mine. But, ever since we'd discovered the word at the bridge, and what it meant, David had used it several times to describe his relationship with his mother. "I told her I'd try an' find you," I said.

David's head bolted up from his arms. "Did you tell'er where I was?"

"No."

"Good."

I could see David's face in the flickering candlelight. His eyes were all puffy and red from crying and there were dirty tear stains running down his cheeks, which alarmed me. I realized that I'd never seen David cry before. Even when he scraped his knee or broke his arm once, jumping off the oil delivery truck barn roof with a red cape on. He didn't cry one tear. "What happened?" I asked.

"Nothin'."

"But..."

"S'none of your business."

"You can't stay here forever."

"Why not?"

"Because. You don't have anything to eat and there's no place to sleep and..."

"You can bring me food and stuff and my sleeping bag."

"But, not forever."

"You're the only one who knows I'm here."

"I know."

"Then, if anyone finds me, I'll know it was you who told and you'll be the one who broke the bond, not me." It wasn't the first time David had used that tactic on me, but something was really bothering him. More than the other times.

"What happened? You can tell me."

David looked at me and absently rubbed his ears; which meant that, whatever had happened had involved an ear-boxing session and, most likely, a visit to the good Reverend Stevens. David looked away from me, then stood up from the table and walked over to a dark corner where the light from the candle didn't reach. I waited in the silence until he finally spoke to me in a low, almost inaudible voice, "She caught me with a stiff in the bathroom."

I immediately knew what he meant. "God," I said,

in a hushed tone, trying to imagine what my mother would say, if she ever caught me with a stiff in our bathroom. "What'd she say?"

There was a long, uncomfortable moment before he answered from the darkness. "She screamed at me that I wasn't her son and that I was disgusting and that I was going to hell."

I'd heard David's mother lose her temper before and could hear her screaming what David was saying. "She really didn't mean it," was all I could manage to say.

"She hates me and she wishes I was dead," came from over in the dark. "I hate'er and I'm never going back there."

"But..."

David walked out of the shadows and stood over the table. The candlelight glowed dramatically up onto his dirty face. But, he wasn't crying. His eyes were firm and cold and there was hardly any color in his face. He stared down at me still seated on the old nail keg. "I'll go back after it gets real dark," he gritted. "I'll wait until she thinks I've been kidnapped and she's real, real scared. That'll teach'er."

I just looked up at David without saying anything. He was not only planning to scare his mother, he was scaring me.

"Are you with me - or against me?" he asked in an almost normal voice. Then, he let me know that, "I didn't tell'er that you do it all the time, too."

"I'm with you," I said. It had only been a few months since David had performed 'the bond' ritual and he was already putting it to the test.

We sat in the clubhouse until well after dark. Then,

when he finally decided the time was right, David raced me all the way back to his house on our bikes. As if nothing had happened. Big Red chose to sleep at my house that night...

...*Patricia... Patricia* stood beside someone. Someone who was taller and dark...who was standing in the shadows... Her expression was fixed. The shadowed person held out his hand. Without any emotion, she placed her hand in his and he led her toward the darkness. Just before she disappeared, she looked around at me... saying nothing. Then, she vanished...

Slowly, the inky darkness gave way to light. A kiss... and another. A bright light pierced my eyes. Big Red licked my face again. I eased him away. Where was I? On my back. In the cottage in Maine with David. On the floor. The broken coffee table on both sides of me. Sandy...where's Sandy? I sat up slowly. Everything hurt. The night's images came shooting at me in volleys of exploding bright flashes in my brain. I shoved the splintered coffee table away from me and pulled myself onto the couch. I reeled to one side and folded over one of the arms. Everything whirled around me... Ira Peak... The knife... Petey... Lady Velma... The demon dog... David... Sandy... Sandy?... "Sandy," I called out hoarsely. I turned my head and looked right into the glaring morning sun that had just reached over the bluff and was streaming in through the living room window, hitting me right in my eyes. I looked around the room. No one. Just Big Red, sitting in the middle of the braided rug. Staring at me with his tongue hanging out.

I shoved myself up onto my feet and lurched to the window. The station wagon was parked outside. So was Sandy's truck. What was it doing there if she wasn't... I looked around and stepped over Big Red and made it to the kitchen doorway. I braced myself against the door frame. No one in the kitchen. I had a terrible thirst and hobbled to the refrigerator, where I took out what was left of the orange juice and gulped half of it down. There was dirt and blood all over the front of my tee-shirt and a dull throbbing ache between my legs. My lips hurt. Where could Sandy be? Where was David? I picked up an opened can of warm beer from the sideboard.

"David," I called out as Big Red whined behind me. I turned and walked stiffly back into the living room. The bedroom door. Closed. The door to the bedroom that David and I were using was closed. David... Where the hell were David and Sandy? I stood in the middle of the living room and upended the rest of the stale beer and dropped the can onto the floor. "Hey, David." No answer. David must have gone to sleep in the bedroom. I tried to open the bedroom door. Locked. The goddamned bedroom door was locked. "Sandy, Sandy?" I banged on the locked door. "Hey, open up," I called. No answer. I heard something. "Sandy? Are you in there?" There was a rustling of sheets and muffled voices from the bedroom. "Sandy?" I called again, staring at the locked door in front of me. I banged on the door. "Hey. Open up." No answer. No sounds.

My head suddenly filled with a blinding red rage... *I'm just glad it was with me...* I reared back and slammed my foot high into the middle of the door. The lock ripped away from the frame. The door flew open and smashed hard against the inside bedroom wall. David's sleeping bag was on the floor. There was a pile of clothes... shoes... David's jeans... Sandy's blouse. A white sheet was pulled up over two bodies on the bed David was using.

"You bastard! You fucking bastard!" I screamed wildly. Nothing moved under the sheet. I spun around, out of control, and ran into the kitchen.

The .22 pistol. I grabbed the gun from the sideboard next to the stove where David had left it and charged back into the living room... *the frog!...the frog!...*

David came hopping out of the bedroom on one foot, frantically trying to pull on his undershorts. My hand aimed the pistol right at his face. A numbing, freezing cold came over me.

David's face contorted. Terrified, he gasped, "God, Billy, don't. Please."

Ice cold tears burst from my eyes. "Liar! Fucking Liar!" I screamed over him. My voice echoed all around me. "Liar! Fucking liar!"

David stammered at me, "No, I didn't... I... for chrissakes, she's just a fuckin' mouth-breather."

I couldn't feel the pistol I held in my hand pointed right at my best friend. "Blood brother!" I screamed.

"We are. We still are," David pleaded. His face was all grayish-white.

"Liar."

Big Red jumped up and started barking.

Suddenly, Sandy came dashing out of the bedroom with the white sheet wrapped around her. She recoiled at the sight of the pistol in my hand. Her scream ricocheted off the walls and through my head. "No! Oh-my-God! No, Billy! Don't!"

"Liar!" I shrieked at her.

Sandy catapulted backwards into the bedroom. Big Red kept barking furiously. I could feel tears of anguish streaming down my face. The gun quivered in my hand. It couldn't be my hand holding the gun.

David was frozen in place, a few feet from the bedroom door. He began to whimper, "Billy, don't... please."

Sandy kept screaming from the bedroom.

"What about the bond?" I blurted out at David. "Huh? What about the sacrifice?"

The buffeting noise, reverberating in my head, came from the bedroom where Sandy was pounding wildly on the window. Trying frantically to open it. "Help me!" she kept screaming. "Somebody, help me!"

My head exploded in a mass of screaming-barking confusion. Someone was holding a gun. It couldn't be me. I couldn't see who was holding the gun pointed at my friend, David. "Tell me about the babies and the cliff," I spit out at David. "Tell me some more of your goddamned stories."

"It's...it's true," David stuttered, "it's all true."

"Liar. All you do is lie. You don't care about anything. You don't give a shit. All you care about is you. You fucking liar. Where's my yellow sand pail?"

David's face was dumbstruck. "What?"

"You stole my yellow sand pail."

Someone's thumb pulled the hammer back on the pistol with a "click." David threw his hands up in front of himself to stop the bullet and screamed. "Oh, God, nooooo! Mom! Mom!" Big Red jumped up and down on his front feet, howling with fear and desperation.

...The ocean roared in through my head and smashed up against the rocks on the small beach at the base of the cliff. Someone was standing where David was standing. It was the black-and-white fiend. Grinning at me. "Do it, Billy..." he seemed to be saying. "Do it. Pull the trigger and kill me... kill me..."

"You don't have any color in your face," I spit out at the fiend in front of me.

"Oh-my-God-oh-my-God," David whimpered pathetically.

...*Patricia...* floated out of the bedroom, wrapped in her white gossamer dress. She floated past the black-and-white fiend. I lowered the pistol that my hand was holding out in front of me. Everything in the room seemed strangely silent... *Patricia* floated right by me toward the front door. Her gossamer dress furled up and away from her nude body, catching the barrel of the pistol, as my hand lowered it down and away from my friend, David...

Big Red let out a sorrowful howl. The sheet pulled the barrel of the gun toward Big Red's head. The hammer struck the shell in the chamber sending the .22 caliber lead bullet tearing into his skull. Big Red spun back in the silence that followed a distant snap of a gunshot. He landed on his haunches and looked at me with a quizzical expression in his eyes. Then, he lost control of his muscles and collapsed to the floor, letting out a sigh as he stopped breathing and quietly closed his eyes.

"Help me!" Sandy screamed from behind me. She was flattened up against the front door. Her eyes were wide. Her hands flailed behind her naked body, trying desperately to find the doorknob. David let out a loud gasp. Sandy flung open the front door and ran outside.

I stared in paralyzed disbelief at Big Red's still form lying in front of me on the braided rug. Slowly, I knelt down beside him and touched his soft, red coat. He looked fine. Maybe, he was just sleeping and was going to wake up. "Oh, no," I whispered. "Oh, God...no..."

I looked up at David, frozen in shock in front of the open bedroom door in his undershorts. Sandy's truck started outside and roared away from the cottage. "Are you happy now?" I asked David, in a voice that seemed not to be mine. My hand rested gently on Big Red's warm head. "Here's your fucking sacrifice." David didn't respond. He couldn't.

My emotions welled up inside me and spilled over. I stood and threw the pistol as hard as I could, right past David's head. It smashed against the wall behind him and dropped to the floor. I spun around and ran crazily out of the cottage.

David had left the keys in the station wagon. I jumped behind the wheel and started the car, then pulled the gearshift down hard into reverse and jammed my foot on the accelerator. My head lurched forward as the rear wheels spun into the gravel. The station wagon lunged backwards and glanced off a tree, smashing the right taillight.

"Billy!" I heard David shout out from the front doorway.

I didn't even look around. My foot stomped on the brake pedal, stopping the car. I shoved the gearshift into drive and stepped on the gas, sending the loose gravel spitting all over David, as I zigzagged away and roared down the dirt road, leaving David standing alone in the doorway with Big Red lying dead inside the cottage. I gripped the steering wheel with one hand and, with my free hand, tried to wipe away the stinging tears that filled my eyes and were nearly blinding me. The station wagon squealed around turn after turn along the back forest roadway. I didn't shoot Big Red. It was an accident... I didn't. I didn't make a sacrifice.

The virgin forest. I hit the brakes hard and ground to a sliding stop next to the broken down entrance to David's 'virgin forest.' The tears in my eyes made the tall dark trees blurry. I wiped my eyes. The forest was quiet. Not a sound. Not even a bird...

...There's only four family names in this whole town... I stepped out of the station wagon and walked over to the stone wall. I paused for a moment and peered into the blackness beyond the trees. *...They're all married to each other...* Liar. *...Which means, they're all interrelated and half crazy...* Fucking liar. *...If you dropped your load in'er and knocked'er up, your kid might come out all fucked-up with a pointy head an' have to be thrown off the cliff...* Liar.

My entire body was trembling. I hurriedly stepped over the low stone wall and walked quickly in between the large pine trees and on into the forest. It seemed much darker than before. I walked faster. Then, broke into a run. Tears filled my eyes again and streamed down my face. *...They throw their deformed babies over the cliff...* "Noooooo!" I ran helter-skelter deeper into the forest. Branches whipped at my face. Suddenly, the big log that David preached from was right in front of me. My shins banged into it and I toppled headlong over the log and slid face-first into the damp blanket of pine needles on the other side.

I don't know how long I lay there. Probably, only a few minutes. I'm not sure. I was so overwhelmed with grief that all my strength had been sapped from my body. Then, I heard something. A short distance off to my left in the forest. A rustling. Voices. "Them city boys don't know when to t'quit."

Jesus-God. Ira Peak. Two men passed by me, only a few yards from where I was laying face-down in the damp pine needles. I held my breath and turned my head ever-so-slightly. Through the tall pines and thick undergrowth, I could just make out Ira Peak and one of his friends. Ira was carrying a shotgun. They stopped for a moment and looked around. I shrank back into myself and hugged the ground until they headed off in another direction. I waited until they'd gone on and I couldn't hear them anymore. Finally, I gathered enough strength to stand up. Ira Peak and his friend had headed away from the direction of the cliff, where David had said they threw away the deformed babies.

...Liar. All my life, I believed you... Suddenly, it didn't matter about Ira and his friend. I didn't care anymore about me. Big Red was dead. I had to find out about the cliff. What if Sandy was pregnant? What if David was telling the truth?

I listened hard to make sure I couldn't hear Ira anymore, and then made my way through the woods toward the cliff. Just as I was about to step out from beyond the trees onto the small strip of dark, scrub-grass covered glacier rock that formed the top of the sheer cliff, my heart froze. I thought I saw something move a few yards off to my right. Maybe, my mind was playing tricks on me. But, I could have sworn I had seen a shadow pull back behind some large pine trees. I stared onto the woods, but saw nothing.

Slowly, I stepped out onto the rock and made my way to the edge of the cliff. I stared down at the narrow, isolated patch of beach below. Just beyond the shoreline, huge waves were crashing violently against the large jagged rocks that protruded angrily up out of the dark sea, as the relentless incoming tide grabbed up more sand in its path.

...This is where they throw away the deformed babies... Right down...there... "I don't believe you. Who told you that?"*...Petey...* "Now, I know you've flipped."*...His cousin is his mother... His cousin is his mother... His cousin is his mother...* David's words ripped through my head. I slapped my hands against my ears, trying to block them out. Tears burst from my eyes. "Stoooop!" I shouted out over the roar of the angry sea. "It's not true! It's all a lie!"

Without thinking, I abruptly dropped to my knees, flipped over onto my belly and let myself down over the edge of the high cliff. I felt around with the toes of my shoes until I found the lip of a narrow ledge and lowered myself down onto it. A wind was beginning to whip up with the incoming tide and sent the spray from the crashing waves up to where I was letting myself down over the ledge. My hand slipped off the damp rock. I grabbed wildly at nothing but air. I felt myself sliding out of control down over the sheer incline to the beach below. In an instant, I landed flat on my back in a thick clump of sea grass that blanketed the top of a sand mound. The wind was knocked out of me. I rolled over onto my stomach and gasped for air.

...This is where they throw the deformed babies... With every incoming wave, the tide was rapidly devouring the small inlet. I had to find out if David was lying. I had to. Still gasping for air, I found myself on my knees, digging

desperately into the wet sand with both hands. The waves pounded the beach, just a few feet away, and sprayed against me. Tears flooded and blurred my vision as I gouged out a hole. If David hadn't lied, maybe Big Red would still be alive.

The faster I dug, the faster water filled the hole, eroding the sides, making it wider instead of deeper. I needed my new yellow sand pail. A large wave crashed onto the beach and lapped up to my pant leg. I dug faster, flailing at the soupy sand. What if I found a...a... *Sometimes, the tide washes away the sand and you can see little white bones sticking up...* The edge of the hole broke away under my knee. I quickly shoved myself back.

...If I fell in, I could fall all the way to China and be eaten by an evil Chinaman... Another wave crashed in and washed right over the hole... *If I fell in I could fall all the way to China and be eaten by an evil Chinaman...*

I snapped my head around in every direction. Where was Big Red? I had to find Big Red before...before... I stood up and bolted back to the bottom of the cliff and started climbing furiously up the jagged face of the glacier rock. Hand over hand. Slipping. Pulling myself back up. Foot after foot, until I reached the lip of the narrow ledge that jutted out just below the top of the cliff, blocking my view. Then, every muscle in my body froze.

"Goddamned little goat turd ain't he'ah. Shit," Ira Peak sputtered from above the ledge. I stopped breathing and flattened myself against the cliff. My heart throbbed in my throat as I listened.

"Whudda you wanna do?" Ira's friend slurred.

Ira uttered, almost to himself, "Jes' gonna make

sur'ah them little smaht-boys know they can't jes' come up he'ah an' poach whatev'ah they want."

Then, a loud gunshot split the air above and sent a load of birdshot down at the beach below. A small round crater exploded in the sand. Then, another blast right beside the first one. I closed my eyes and dug my fingers into the rock... *Please, God, don't let the evil Chinaman get me...* Please, David, don't let them get me...

"Come on, we'll look aroun' awhile long'ah. Damn cah's he'ah. Gotta be he'ah abouts." I heard them both shuffle back into the woods and Ira muttered, "Damned Sandy-girl ain't goin' nowhe'ah!"

Slowly, I let some air quietly seep into my lungs and waited until all I could hear were the waves crashing below. I looked down and saw the two foot-wide holes Ira had blasted out of the sand. Water was rapidly filling them in from beneath the surface. Something was protruding up from the middle of one of them. Something small... and white... like... like... small white...

My grip began to give way. I quickly grabbed onto the ledge above me and pulled myself up onto it gasping for breath. I turned to look back down at the hole with the small white... The sea had filled it in. A wave washed up and quickly dissolved it into a sandy dimple. Nothing more.

With every ounce of strength left in me, I climbed the last few feet and pulled myself up onto the top of the cliff; where I just lay flat and let my eyes close and my mind drift before I started back into the forest. Had David told me the truth? Did I see something in the sandy hole?...

..."How old is Big Red, anyway?"

"About thirteen or fourteen, I think. When did you get'im?”

"When you were almost two and me three, I think, why?"

"That's pretty old in dog years."

"How old?"

"I think it's seven dog years for every man year, or somethin' like that."

"That would make him about...Geez. Over ninety years old."

"Yeah, somethin' like that."

"But, he doesn't act ninety. He looks just like he always looks. How long do dogs live?"

"I dunno."...

...How long do dogs live?...How long do dogs live?... How long to dogs live?... Sandy, stop screaming... How long do dogs live?... Sandy, stop screaming... I can't find Big Red. Where's Big Red? I can't see Big Red from way up here on the whale rock... He's too far away... He can't hear me screaming for him. Big Red, come back. Big Red. Coooomebaaaak!...

...The shotgun blast from the hunter's rifle cracked through the trees. I heard Big Red's yelp and dropped my bicycle at the side of the old farm road. Big Red wasn't supposed to be in the woods. It was hunting season and David was supposed to keep Big Red inside or over at the oil delivery truck barn until the hunters were out of the woods. I ran and ran through the trees. David had promised that he'd keep an eye on Big Red; but like always, he was in too much of a hurry to get to Vic's pepper steak shop and left his back door open. Big Red was in the woods, trying to find one of us. Heading for our secret clubhouse.

The woods grew dark and the trees hovered over me. I heard a noise and ducked behind a tree. The hunter came thrashing in my direction. The black-and-white demon hunter. He strode right by without looking at me. I felt an autumn chill rush by with him. Then, I heard a feeble whine, just up ahead, and ran toward it. It was getting darker in the woods. Big Red hobbled and weaved back along the path leading to our secret club house. He stopped and fell over on his side with a mournful cry. I ran to him and knelt down. There was dark blood on his red coat, just below his rib cage. He was still alive, but unconscious. I picked him up in my arms and hurried as fast as I could back along the path, out of the woods to the road where I'd left my bike. I wasn't able to ride and hold onto big Red at the same time; so I carried his limp body all the way to the dog and cat hospital and waited for two hours, until the doctor came out of the operating room and told me that they'd gotten all of the birdshot out and that Big Red would be okay in a few weeks. I called David's house and told his mother what'd happened. David wasn't home...

I woke with a start, screaming for Big Red as loud as I could. I was lying flat on my stomach near the edge of the cliff. The sun was beating down on me from above. I looked up at the thick pines of the virgin forest looming overhead, just a few feet in front of me. Everything hit me at once. Everything that'd happened. All of it. I sprang to my feet and ran as fast as I could into the woods.

Maybe, Big Red wasn't dead. Maybe, he was just

wounded, like before, and David needed me back at the cottage to help get Big Red to a hospital. Maybe, David never lied to me ever in his life. Maybe, Sandy really was just a stupid mouth-breather after all. Just like David said and...and...

I stopped short. Someone was coming toward me. Two men. Ira Peak and his friend. They were coming back after me. I could just make them out, as they hurried in between the tall pines about fifty yards away. I didn't know where to hide. They were coming straight for me!

The hand shot out from behind a large pine tree that grew up out of a thick cluster of elderberry bushes, and clamped tightly over my mouth. It jerked me back so hard that I heard my neck bones pop. Someone had grabbed me and was holding me against them down behind the big tree, hidden from view by the thick elderberry bushes. The hand was so firmly clamped over my mouth that I could hardly breathe. Then, the smell hit me. The musky odor of cheap men's cologne.

"I know I heared someone holl'ah back this way," Ira Peak rasped, as he walked right up to the other side of the tree and stopped. I heard him stick the barrel of his shotgun into the elderberry bushes and swish it around. The hand clamped over my mouth pressed tighter.

"Shit," Ira muttered at not finding me.

"Maybe, he be back over t'tha cliff," Ira's friend suggested with a lisping twang.

"He best not let me find'im' the'ah." They started back through the brush. "Who told'im 'bout these woods anyways? Petey's gonna pay if he been runnin' his mouth," Ira said menacingly as they thrashed off into the forest, heading back in the direction of the cliff.

Slowly, I felt the pressure of the tight grip over my mouth begin to relax. I was so petrified with fear that it took me several moments before I could move my head around. But, the odor of the cheap men's cologne lessened the shock of turning to look right into the horribly scarred eye of Cyrus Peak the cripple.

He let me go. I stepped back, facing him. Not able to say a word. Cyrus just stared at me with the forever paralyzed expression on his face. Except, there was something... something deep within his sighted eye that told me more. I saw the atrophied muscles beneath Cyrus' scarred, blotchy face tighten noticeably. Straining hard. He was trying to tell me something. His small slash of a mouth twisted as he attempted to form a word. No sound emitted, except a slight wheeze of escaping air. Without thinking, I stepped closer. His facial muscles contorted again. I put my ear up close to his mouth and could feel his sour breath on my cheek. His breath became a whisper. The whisper rattled into a word. "Go!"

I stepped back and looked at Cyrus for a very long moment. Then, I nodded my thanks to him for having saved my life. In the instant that I turned away to leave him behind, I saw the glint of a small tear tip from the fragile, ragged tissue surrounding his eye and run down his distorted mask. And, I ran.

I stood in the quiet that surrounded the cottage. A slight breeze had begun to sift in through the tall green pine trees, causing my whirligig-bird prize to whirl its wings around on the end of its stick. It was the only thing I could find to place as a symbol on Big Red's grave.

When I had arrived back at the cottage, the black-

and-white fiend just stood in the background and watched, politely staying out of the way; but watching nonetheless, as I drifted through the motions of helping repair and clean up the cottage before we drove back home. I don't remember who washed the dark blot off the braided rug in the living room. I think it was me. But, maybe, it was both of us. I do remember how Big Red was buried, though. David quietly dug a large hole next to a big pine that Big Red had staked out as his primary spritzing tree, and I carefully laid him down into it. While David was covering him up, I went back into the cottage and, without a word, picked up the .22 pistol, took it outside and threw it as far as I could off into the woods.

Through it all, I don't think we even looked at each other - except for once. We'd both spotted the wadded up white sheet at the same time. It was lying half-hidden behind a tree next to where Sandy's pickup truck had been parked. David retrieved it and shoved it into the covered garbage hole at the side of the cottage, while I said good-bye to Big Red.

I stayed by Big Red's grave for quite awhile, as David loaded the station wagon. I know I cried some and I could feel the presence of the black-and-white monster nearby. But, I didn't care. The demon didn't scare me anymore. This was between Big Red and me. I was saying "good-bye" to a very special friend.

As we drove down through the town for the last time, we both continued our silence and looked straight ahead. Neither of us acknowledged the sight of Petey Peak sitting slumped alone on the edge of the wooden sidewalk in front of the general store, staring vacantly off at nothing in particular. I did, however, catch sight of the dark silhouette of a hunched over figure framed inside the grimy store window. I was sure he was wearing a cheap men's cologne to help himself remember that, at the very least, he had tried to get out.

I wasn't even tempted to look back, as we ascended the bluff that overlooked the town. It all seemed so distant and unreal. But, the twinge of fear that stabbed me in the pit of my stomach, when I spotted the rabid 'demon dog' as it hobbled out from behind the weathered WELCOME TO PEAKSPORT sign, was very real. And, I knew that the unsettled feeling it gave me inside would be with me for a long time to come. I rested my head back on the seat and closed my eyes. We were leaving the land of the mouth-breathers behind forever.

I'm not sure how long we'd been driving, when David pulled off the highway to buy gas. But, from the surrounding terrain and the several familiar roadside businesses haphazardly strung along next to each other, it must have been a couple of hundred miles, at least. David got out of the station wagon and began filling the tank. I realized that, during the three or four hours we'd been on the road, I hadn't spoken a word and not one thought had entered my head.

I opened my door, got out of the car and headed for the men's room off to the side of the small white two-pump gas station.

Having relieved myself in the cramped cubicle, I stood at the dirty washbasin with its dripping faucet. The mirror in front of me had a crack running through it from top to bottom that separated the glass about a quarter of an inch, causing my reflection to be distorted with one-half of my face slightly higher than the other. The image of myself with my head split in two fascinated me somehow. With the crack having dissected my head into two sections, it was the first time that I'd noticed that one side of my face wasn't exactly the same as the other side. In fact, as I leaned in closer, I could see that the two sides of me were actually very different people. The eye that looked back at me from the left side of my head was slightly smaller and didn't seem to have quite as much expression in it as the right one. Also, my left eye was a shade lighter brown than my right. Not so much that anyone would notice, but a shade lighter just the same. My mouth, too, said something different, depending on which side of the cracked mirror I studied. The lips on the left side of my mouth were thinner and followed a narrow straight line into my cheek. The right side had a slight curve up at the corner that could almost be interpreted as the beginning of a smile.

There were other subtle differences; but I backed off and adjusted my stance, so that I could see myself in only one-half of the cracked mirror. The cut in my head was only superficial and was mostly hidden by my hair. I touched my bottom lip. It still had a noticeable split in it, but the swelling had subsided to a point where I wouldn't have to do much explaining to my mother. It was what I couldn't see on the surface of my reflection, but could feel beneath my expression that was affecting me the most... *I'm just glad it was with me...* The black-and-white fiend slipped quietly into the small bathroom and stood behind me, staring over my shoulder, as I leaned back into my reflected divided eyes in the cracked mirror. We didn't speak, as my thoughts came flooding over me. Could I have really shot David? Could I have killed my best friend since birth? Just because I caught him in bed with some girl I'd only known for two days. The black-and-white monster stood behind me in my reflection... waiting for my answer... It had been my finger on the trigger. But, I had already lowered the gun before the sheet had pulled the barrel toward Big Red. Still, it was my finger that had squeezed the trigger. I couldn't deny that... *the frog! the frog!...*

I turned away from the mirror and opened the door to the small men's room. As I started to step out into the light, I stopped and looked back into the cracked mirror. The black-and-white monster was gone. I walked out into the daylight and closed the door behind me.

The station wagon turned the corner onto Chestnut Street where I lived. I noticed that the leaves on the ancient elm tree, that stood guard out in front of my family's white Cape Cod home, had turned yellow and deep gold. Had they already turned before I'd left on the trip or during the days I was away?

The station wagon pulled up in front of my house and stopped. Big Red was late. Whenever David and I went anyplace for any length of time, Big Red would usually choose to stick around my house; because he somehow knew that would be the first place the station wagon would stop when we returned, and he would come running out to greet us.

We both sat encased in a dreadful silence. Both of us wanting to speak and both with nothing to say. I got out of the car and walked around to the back, opened the rear hatch and retrieved my sleeping bag and small suitcase. Then, just as I started to close the hatch, I caught the faint smell of 'nature's perfume.' I quickly closed the hatch and started up the walkway to the front door of my house.

"Hey! I'll see-ya later, huh?" David said, hopefully, from behind the wheel of the station wagon.

I stopped, but didn't turn around. "I'm sorry about Big Red," I managed to say.

"Oh-hey," David called out too quickly, his voice shaking noticeably. "It's okay. He was gettin' old anyway, ya-know? I mean, he was just a dog anyway, right? Hey, it wasn't even your fault. I saw the sheet pull the..."

I was standing on the flagstone walkway to my house, with my back to David, a few feet from the curb where he was parked in the station wagon. I turned. "He was Big Red," I said, interrupting him in a flat monotone.

"I know-I know," David stammered, "but-but, I...I mean, we can get another dog just like'im, Right?"

David knew he had my attention and was making an end run. "I gotta go," I said and started to turn away.

"Look, we'll just say that we got rear-ended by one of those stupid jerks and Big Red jumped outta the car and got hit by a truck, right? That's all we gotta say. That way, I can explain what happened to the taillight and you can tell what happened to your lip. That's all we gotta say, right?"

A very heavy sadness suddenly leaped into my chest. I looked up at the elm tree, with its turning leaves, and at the puffs of white clouds that were rolling in with the dusk. I thought of my grandfather. He once told me about a distant relative, tried as a witch for committing adultery, who was supposedly hung from the very same tree.

David's voice snapped me back. "Hey, look," he went on, sounding like nothing had happened and everything was as it was before we'd left. As if he was, somehow, back in control of the situation. "We gotta start throwin' the football around. Tryouts are next week an' we gotta be ready, right?"

I'd never lied to David. I always told him everything... except... except for... "I...I'm not going out for football," I said in a low voice.

Without looking over at David, I knew the expression on his face. It would be the same as always, whenever he felt he was being wronged. A quizzical, hurt look, as if he alone was the one being persecuted and not the one responsible for the predicament he found himself in.

"But...but... what about our plan? I...I'm gonna be the quarterback and you're gonna be my end, right?"

I paused, then looked over at him. I was right about his hurt expression. "I took an exam to go away to prep school," I said.

David's face flushed red. "But...but... you didn't tell me..." he uttered in disbelief and nervously cleared his throat.

It was right then that I realized I couldn't remember ever having seen David's face getting beet red like mine before. Never. In fact, whenever he'd gotten really angry or embarrassed, or trapped himself in a situation where he was in the middle of a big lie and was having difficulty getting out of it, he would usually turn very pale. Sometimes almost gray, like a color photograph that had nearly faded to black and white.

"You never told me," he went on, as real tears

began to well in his eyes, "You never told me you were going away to school."

My heart was beginning to hurt. I found myself fighting hard to keep the overwhelming sadness inside of me from spilling over. "My parents took me for an interview last month to see if I'd like it. They think it would help me get into a good college."

David's eyes became desperate. "But...but, you don't really have to go, right? I mean, they're not making you go, right?"

I hesitated, then said, "It's up to me."

"Good," David gushed in a rush of relief. "Then, it's okay. You don't have to go. Fuck, you really scared the shit out of me for a..."

"I'm going."

Instinctively, David tried to smile, but his mouth contorted and more moisture gathered in his eyes. He quickly switched gears and tried to laugh it off. "But-hey, we always said we'd tell each other everything an' stuff, right? I mean, that's not gonna change, huh?"

The heaviness inside of me wouldn't let up. David's voice rose in pitch, as he grasped at anything that might turn the inevitable away, "I...I mean, what about the bond? We've still got the bond, haven't we?"

...A bond is about to pass between us... A bond that no one will ever be able to take away from us... Blood brothers...

I had to look away again. The elm tree was blurred, but I didn't wipe away the tears filling my eyes.

David made a sudden move inside the station wagon. I looked at him. He'd opened the glove compartment and was hurriedly rummaging around in all the road maps, rock tapes, and junk, looking for something. I watched, as he frantically pulled out what looked like his old scout knife. He fumbled nervously with it and opened the blade. It was his old scout knife. David turned and looked at me through the opened window of the station wagon. His eyes were wide and round. His face had flushed from beet red to grayish-white. His words rolled out of his mouth in a rapid, uncontrolled stammer. "Hey. W-we can do it a-again," he babbled, as he thrust both of his hands out through the window at me. One hand held the scout knife with the large blade opened. His other hand extended his thumb. "We can make the bond-of-friendship again; so-so we'll always be blood brothers. Right? No matter what. Right?"

In the next instant, before I could move or utter a word, David had pierced his thumb with the scout knife. He held it out to me, his eyes pleading in desperation. "Come on, Billy... Come on." His face was almost pure white. "Hey, you don't have to cut yours...just...just..." He quickly tossed the opened scout knife back into the station wagon. His voice choked to a whisper, as he extended his bleeding thumb out as far as it would reach, "Please." His blood dripped onto the flagstone walkway.

I hesitated for a moment, then strangely, I felt myself being drawn toward him, until I was standing right in front of David's extended thumb. I tried desperately to suppress the flood that was ready to burst the dam within me. David's eyes were red-rimmed and brimming with tears. "Please," he pleaded.

I slowly held up my thumb. David quickly grasped it and pressed his bleeding thumb to mine with his other hand, clutching them tightly together for a long moment, as he looked deeply into my eyes. At that moment, I felt the strike of a lightning bolt and realized just how fragile a person my friend David really was.

As he held fast to our thumbs, a smile began to ease across David's ashen face. His tears receded. He released our thumbs, turned and gripped the steering wheel firmly with both hands. Staring straight ahead, through the bug-splattered windshield, he uttered reassuringly to himself, "Okay. Everything's okay, now." He looked back at me. "Right? Everything's okay now, right?"

I didn't respond, so David responded for me. "Right," he confirmed and started the car. "Okay," he said with an exaggerated sigh of relief in his voice that blocked out any acceptance of what was really happening. "I'll see you around, right? I mean, I'll see you around," he underscored with a forced grin.

I looked at him, but didn't acknowledge his statement. I couldn't.

Then, in his own way, David gunned the station wagon's engine and squealed away from the curb. I stood there and watched him roar down the tree-lined street and take the far corner in a leaning, rubber-burning skid and disappear from view. I waited where I stood, until I heard the distant report of the backfire. Then, still holding everything inside of me, I picked up my sleeping bag and suitcase and walked up the flagstone walkway to my front door. Without looking back, I went inside and closed the door behind me. Walked upstairs to my bedroom, buried my face in my pillow, and cried quietly for a long time. I had done what David had always wanted me to do. I had finally made my own... sacrifice.

EPILOGUE

Summer - Peaksport, Maine

Dear Bill,

Well, here we are way up in Maine. Finally, after all these years of saying that we would take a real vacation someday, I was able to get your father out of his office (and me away from everyone else in town) to take up the standing offer to use this wonderful little cottage. Fred Pingree - you remember him - he's the real estate agent friend of ours, who shares your father's office downtown. He rents it out for David. Although, I think finding out that David has it on the market hastened our decision.

Now that we're here, I can't imagine why we waited so long. I guess it took Dad all this time to make sure every man, woman, and child in our town was adequately insured and me to realize that I am not Mother Teresa. Anyway, we made it and now I'm going to keep my promise to myself to sit down and write you a very, very long letter. So, my dear, you will have to just bear with me while I ramble on.

As you can see, by the picture postcard I've enclosed, this quaint little town probably hasn't changed very much since you and David drove up here when you were teenagers. Now, I know why you were so secretive about it. Who would want the outside world to find such a pristine place? They would just come up here in droves and ruin it.

There aren't many people here, just a few artist types and the locals, who are rather shy and quiet. Although, the ones we've met seem very nice. Maybe, it's just me, but it feels like time just stopped here sometime ago.

After we arrived and got ourselves settled, we drove into town to get a few things and met this very charming young man who works at the little general store. His name is Eben. He said it means "rock." Anyway, we asked him if he had any tips on what sights to see and he immediately volunteered to be our tour guide today, since business was slow at the store and the owner, who is his cousin, (a very nice, but awfully shy, crippled man) said it was alright. Of course, Dad offered to pay Eben for his trouble, but he wouldn't hear of it. I think he was just bored and wanted to get out of the store for awhile.

Well, first, Eben insisted on taking us on a long walk through a nearby forest that he most appropriately described as a "virgin forest." All I can say is, it absolutely defies description it's so beautiful. Once we got beyond the first rows of trees, it was just like walking into a fairyland. We ended up on top of a high cliff that looks down onto a solitary inlet where the waves came smashing in on the rocks so hard that we could barely hear ourselves talking. Eben told us that the story is, it's the place where angels come to die.

Then, the three of us drove about ten miles up to a spot near the top of a mountain that I must tell you is one of the most breathtaking sights I've ever seen! Just off the road, there's an enchanting field covered entirely by snow-white daisies and surrounded by white birch trees. Right in the middle of it is a big gray rock that looks just like the nose of a giant whale coming up out of the ocean. Eben told us it's his "screaming place." He actually (you have to imagine this, dear) got me to stand up on top of the whale rock with him and shout as loud as we could. Naturally, your father thought it was silly and wouldn't do it, but I must admit, it really was fun and I felt quite exhilarated. Also, the view from up on the rock is utterly fantastic. It almost seems as if you can see forever.

On the way back, Eben told us all about himself and his mother. It seems that, just after he was born, some crazy drunken man broke into their home and tried to kill them both! Fortunately, she has a cousin named Petey who was there at the time and shot the intruder with a pistol he'd found in the woods. Then, it seems, that Eben's mother wanted so much for him to have an education that she drove right up to the Governor's office in Augusta and demanded that a new school be built to replace the one that burned down. They must have listened to her, because Eben's going off to college in the fall. He told us that he scored one of the highest grades on the college entrance exams in the state and has been awarded a full scholastic scholarship to U of Maine. He's very proud of the fact that he will be the first person from around here to go on to college. He says he owes it all to his mother, who used to take him on the train to Boston every year to see the sights. She seems like quite a woman. I'm sorry we won't get to see her. She owns and runs two lobster boats and a shrimp trawler and is much too busy. Eben says that she's doing quite a lobster and shrimp business and is also planning to buy this very cottage we're staying in. He didn't mention anything about his father, but he must be a very nice person to have such a lovely - and I must say quite handsome - son. When he found out the cottage didn't have a television set, he insisted that we borrow an old one they use in the general store. It's one of those very old black-and-white portables with rabbit ears, but, as long as Dad has his sports and his news, he's in heaven. (I can sneak in my favorite soap, too.)

I'm sorry if I've rambled on here, but I warned you that this was going to be a long letter and, knowing me, when I get back home, I probably won't waste any time getting right back into being much too busy to write.

There is one very sad note that I feel I must tell you about. Just before we left, something quite dreadful happened. One of David's twin boys had a terrible accident. It seems that they both got into David's gun collection and took real guns out into the woods to play army with. From what I understand, one of the guns was one of those illegal automatic types and was loaded. I wasn't able to contact David or his mother, but the story around town is that, even though he will live, the poor child may be crippled for life. But, we can hope for the best.

We did send a card and I think you should, too. After all, you were once very good buddies and, in time of need, it's good to hear from old friends. We'll try to pay a visit to his mother, since she's all alone now. After David's father passed away, she became quite reclusive. She still lives in the house across the street from the fuel business, but we hardly see her anymore - not even in church.

David has been running the business, but all those nasty rumors keep circulating about all the goings-on with some sort of sleazy group he and his wife keep company with. I keep getting mixed up as to which one of those girls from All Saints he married. Really doesn't matter, I guess. But, the rumors have caused the business to slip considerably. You know how these little New England towns can be. Rumors beget rumors.

It's funny how you just assume a person is going to turn out the way they're supposed to. I remember how excited and imaginative David always seemed about everything, and how both you boys and that big red dog used to race around all over the place. But, after you went off to school and then to college, David just seemed to fade out of our lives.

By the way, just so you won't hear it from someone else, Reverend Stevens is no longer minister of our church. He and his wife are divorced and the elders felt everyone would be better off if he just quietly left. Actually, they wanted to sweep the sordid details under the rug as quickly as possible. We heard that he moved all the way out to Las Vegas and opened one of those instant marriage chapels.

One last thing. Dad says "thank you" for sending that very generous check. You needn't have. We never meant that money as a loan. We just assumed you needed it to get you through your college years. Of course, we did wonder, at times, if our son happened to be the most expensive college student in history. And, as it turns out, the most responsible. Naturally, I am prejudiced. Anyway, thanks. Maybe, we'll just use some of it to buy us a round-trip ticket to Chicago around Christmastime.

Well, enough. I have to cook Dad and me an early supper. Eben has invited us to a barn dance tonight and tomorrow I understand there's a carnival coming to town.

Love, Mom

P.S. I'm very proud of you getting that big promotion. But, I always knew your company would make the right choice. Just imagine, our son on the 100th floor of the tallest building in Chicago. Dad sends his congratulations and liked your joke about holding the highest office in the USA next to God. However, he says he'll stick to insuring cars and houses in our hometown. He thinks that insuring space satellites is too risky. But, remember, he wouldn't stand up on top of the whale rock either. Love and kisses to Patricia and the kids.

...There's a time, very early in the morning, when I am all alone in our bathroom, staring at my reflection in the mirror over the washbasin. There's no crack in this mirror to divide my face into two parts. No black-and-white fiend lurking behind me. The mirror is clean and spotless with no distortions. Only the truth in what I see looking back at me. And, in those few quiet moments, I can look directly into my own eyes and know what I know...

Other than seeing him from a distance now and then, I only spoke with David one other time after I went away to school. It was during a brief vacation in my final year of college. One of the few times I returned home, as it turned out. He just dropped by our house unannounced. Naturally, my father was at his insurance office downtown and mother was at her volunteer post at the community hospital. So, it was just David and me, and a football game droning on the TV set in our den.

He'd never made quarterback. Never even went out

for football, for that matter. And, by choice, neither had I. He hadn't changed much. Heavier, but still David. But, it was his eyes that particularly caught my attention. They had lost the sparkling snap I'd remembered and had settled into a permanent, and rather lurid, squint, as if they had seen too much of a good thing. He told me, rather matter-of-factly, that his father had installed him across the street from the family home, as the fuel oil sales manager and truck dispatcher, with the idea that he would take over the business when his father retired.

He'd married Margaret, one of the All Saints girls. I wasn't sure whether it was the one Patricia had seen leaning on my shoulder in the Orpheum passion pit, or the other one, until David pulled a well-worn, quite suggestive photo out of his wallet. Naturally, of the two girls David had played around with, Margaret was the one with the largest breasts. As I handed the photo back to him, without comment, he intimated to me that they were into some "pretty neat things" and that Margaret had been his favorite all along. I could only wonder what kind of life they had in store for them and what their kids would turn out to be like. David also inferred that, had I been in town, he would have used me as his best man at his wedding. But, seeing that I wasn't around, he didn't use one.

David asked me if I wanted to come over to see the house he had built on the acre of land next door to the fuel yard that his father had given him as a wedding present. He wanted me to stay for dinner and, since I didn't have a date, he'd get their friend Mary to come over, too. The other half of the pair of gum-snappers, I recalled. She wasn't married and the three of them still hung around together like the old days. I begged off, saying I was leaving for Greece the next morning on a student exchange program and wouldn't be back for quite some time. His attempt at enticing me with the knowledge that good old Mary was “a really fun time” didn't tempt me. In fact, it'd made me think seriously about trying to catch an earlier flight.

We were kind of quiet for the next few minutes. Both of us watching the football game. Neither of us knowing what the score was. Then, David looked over at me with the darkest expression I'd ever seen on his face. An expression that I've never forgotten. His eyes had become eerily detached with an almost transcendental cast to them. His skin had grown as pale as white chalk and the voice that came out of him was low and flat, as he bluntly accused me of forgetting who my real friend was. Then, he stood up, turned his back on me and left without saying a word.

I sat alone in the den listening and heard him slam his car door and roar away from my house. Subconsciously, I waited for the sound of the backfire. It didn't come.

The view from my office window in Chicago, on the 100th floor of one of the tallest buildings in the world, is something to behold. Especially at the magic moment, just before dusk brings on the evening and the lights over a thousand feet below me start to twinkle on, like so many fireflies making their way around The Loop. Standing right up next to the floor to ceiling window, I understand how much of a climb it has been to reach... the highest office in the USA next to God. To be able to stand alone and look out at the glorious panorama sends a thrill through my body because, at some point in my climb, I was able to mend the crack in the mirror that divided my reflection and join the two parts together into one.

That's why I try to continue to think about David now and then, as I have just done, and why it is that I remember it all - every single instance from beginning to end. Every picture comes back crystal clear as if I was right there experiencing it all over again. And, I do. But, each time, I remember just a bit more, interpreting something new in the recollection that adds a fresh dimension that I may not have entirely understood before. Evoking an emotion that triggers a new consideration of what I, heretofore, had felt was chiseled in stone. And, each time, I come away from my time spent with David with a sadness and melancholy. Because, in my musings, David is still David. Doing what David wants. Whenever he wants to, and only on his terms. So, I yield that to David, mindful that, when he does return to me, he will come loaded for bear. Roaring right at me in his 'high-charge.' Shouting to the heavens above, "I want to know everything about everything."

The difference is that I now understand David for what he is and acknowledge that for all his failings, he paid a hefty price. That summer 'going down Maine' changed our lives forever. It pushed me toward something better. That was David's gift to me and, his personal... sacrifice.

From where I stand, I look out over the splendid expanse of Lake Michigan. It is so clear that it seems as if I can see for a million miles and beyond. All the way to the tip of a whale rock that bursts up out of an ocean of flowing white daisies, and I am ever-so-tempted to scream my fool head off... to hear my voice reverberate beyond the ring of birch trees, down over the green forest and lap up against the far-off mountain range as it echoes on into the horizon.

I listen closely, in the surrounding silence, until I can hear the faint tinkling of bicycle bells and the shouts of two best friends, as they race along a back country road, with their bathing suits flapping from their handlebars... "Hey, Big Red!" they shout together, "Come on! Come on, boy!" And, a young red dog snaps his head around and charges through a field of summer wildflowers, then leaps an ancient stone wall... built a long time ago by Paul Revere.

ACKNOWLEDGEMENTS

There are three individuals who had a direct influence on this novel and its publication. First and foremost, Melinda Riccilli Slade for her rare talents for organization, research, professionalism, and unwavering support – and for making sure I was able to stay on point. Editing a novel can be difficult at best. However, if the editor is knowledgeable and skilled at understanding what the author's vision is, and is able to bring clarity to the story, then the battle is well worth it. These are the unique attributes that Melinda brought to this project and I am eternally grateful.

A deep appreciation goes to Morgan Riccilli Slade for his exceptional artistic eye and for his interpretation and execution of the cover photography and artwork, as well as for designing and execution of the novel's website.

A very special thank you to Mitchel Slade for his constant encouragement, and for making sure that we had the up-to-date capabilities to help bring *Going Down Maine* to fruition. -- And, to all three for being who you are.

ABOUT THE AUTHOR

Mark Slade was born Mark Van Blarcom Slade in Salem, Massachusetts. An award-winning actor and writer, he spent thirty years in the entertainment industry.

He currently resides in the San Francisco Bay area with his wife Melinda, where he continues to pursue his artistic endeavors.

"Going Down Maine" is his first novel.

For further biographical information:
www.goingdownmaine.com
www.markladestudio.com
www.imdb.com
www.wikipedia.org

23036766R00138

Printed in Great Britain
by Amazon